HOOD SUPREME 3

MZ. LADY P

MZ. LADY P PRESENTS, LLC

Hood Supreme 3

Copyright © 2020 by Mz. Lady P
Published by Mz. Lady P Presents

This is a work of fiction. Any references or similarities to actual events, real people, living or dead, or to the real locals intended to give the novel a sense of reality. Any similarity in other names, characters, places, and incidents are entirely coincidental.

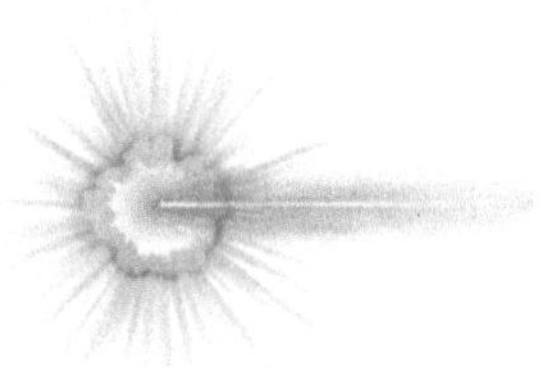

Melissa and India roughly pushed the two women as they all walked inside of the garage. Luckily, for us, they forgot to close the door. Silk and I slowly crept inside of the garage. I swear these were some of the stupidest criminals I've ever seen. They had made some rookie ass mistakes. They hadn't locked the door that led from the garage to the inside of the house.

"If any of these motherfuckers' act like they want smoke, give it to them!" Silk spoke through gritted teeth. He didn't have to tell me because I already had it in my mind that I was killing them.

As we walked inside the house, I could hear Melissa's aggravating ass voice. It was about to be the highlight of my life putting a bullet in the bitch's head. We stopped and listened to her conversation.

"Why the fuck would you bring them here? I don't need that heat over here."

"Really, Butch! Have you been watching the news? The Roebucks were gunned down tonight outside of Blackbird. I know them motherfuckers coming for us next. I just need to lay low here until my pilot can get us to the Dominican Republican. I have buyers for them over there. They've already sent the deposit. All I have to do is get them sold, and I'm in the clear. No one will ever know about this shit!"

"I can't believe you've been holding Chanel and her daughter hostage all of these years. I should never have let you talk me into this shit."

"You should have thought about that before you started fucking her. It's not my fault your aim is off and she survived!

"No! What you should have done was left her in the hospital in the coma? Her sons are going to murder y'all ass when they found out what you did. That janky ass hospital and the government all had a hand in her kidnapping. All I want to do is have a relationship with my daughters Miyani and India! I didn't sign up for this other shit.

"What the fuck?" I said in a low tone.

The wheels in my head started to turn as I rushed through the house, trying to find the women they had just brought in the house.

"Slow down, Prada!" I could hear Silk say behind me, but I couldn't stop. Seeing India step out of a room made me jump back so that she wouldn't see me. Once she was out of sight, I rushed to the door and opened it. I fell to my knees, looked at my mother chained to the other woman. I didn't know if this was a nightmare or a dream come true.

"This shit can't be real!"

"What have they done to you, ma?" I moved her hair from her face and she locked eyes with me.

"Prada baby, is that you?"

Chanel Alexander

My mind raced as I looked at my son Prada. I never in a million years thought that I would see one of my precious boys again. Staring into his tearful eyes hurt me, but I couldn't cry at the moment. It was as if time was standing still. Looking at Silk with tears streaming down his face was too much but familiar. The last time I saw him, he was crying because he caught me in bed with Butch. Back then, I was playing a dangerous ass game. That game got me where I am right now.

"Stop crying and grab those keys before they come back!" Clearly, I had to get in control of this situation. They were bawling their eyes out, and I needed them to man the fuck up right now. I've definitely been gone for too long because they know I don't play that crying shit.

"I'm about to murder all them motherfuckers!" Prada jumped up and got ready to head out of the room we were.

"Right now, you have to get us out of these chains and out of here. This shit is bigger than you think. The keys are over there on that hook! Stop all of that fucking crying, Silk! You know I hate that shit. I need y'all to focus right now."

As weak as I was, I needed to be the strong one right now. I've waited for years to get out of this situation. This was the chance to get out and fuck up every person that had something to do with my kidnapping and torture. Looking over at my daughter Versace, I knew she was more than ready. For a long time, she lived a normal life while we were in captivity, never really knowing that we were hostages of the government. Shit was good until Butch got out of jail, and Melissa became jealous once again.

Without hesitation, Prada sprang into action, grabbing the keys while Silk stood with his gun aimed toward the door. The moment my wrists became free, I jumped up and started helping free my daughter.

"Why can't we kill them right now?"

"If we kill them, then I'll never be able to murder every motherfucker who had a hand in this shit. Get us out of here now! Shoot only if you have to!" I sternly spoke as I grabbed my son's face.

"This baby is coming, ma!" Looking over at my daughter, I knew we needed to hurry up.

Silk quickly scooped her up, and we rushed out of the garage. The whole time them silly bitches were arguing. It was game the fuck on! Chanel Alexander is back, and it's time for a lot of people to pay the fucking queen.

ONE

PRADA

"Prada, baby, please have a seat and stop pacing like that!" Gavin said.

"How the fuck can I stop pacing? In case your ass forgot, the mother I thought was dead is very much alive. Not only is she alive, but she didn't allow us to murk the motherfuckers who did this shit to her. I swear I'm going to murk your bitch ass momma. Just stop talking to me right now, cause you pissing me the fuck off!" I didn't mean to go off on Gavin the way that I was, but I was heated.

"I can't believe you and Silk went without hitting Fendi

and me up. All those motherfuckers would be dead right now!" G yelled as he kicked over the coffee table.

"Hold on now! I'm just as upset as you boys are, but don't break my shit up! This shit is not making sense to me at all. If my daughter is alive, then who the fuck is that on the mantle in the urn?" We all looked over at the mantle at the fucking urn we had basically lived our lives mourning over.

"None of this shit is adding up! She's been alive all of this time. Hell, she's even given birth to a daughter. Something is not right, and them doctors need to hurry the fuck up. Damn Prada! You should have called us before meeting up with Silk. This shit is so foul!" Fendi gritted, and that was it.

"Man, fuck this shit! Come on, Gavin!" I grabbed her ass and forcibly made her ass walk out of my grandma's house. These motherfuckers were pissing me off, and I was over it.

"Slow down before you make me fall! Please calm down. You're scaring me. All of this shit is scaring me, Prada!"

"Right now, I can't pacify your emotions. Unless you missed the memo, my mother has been held hostage by your mother. Let's not make this about you right now!"

Once we were both in the car, I pulled off like a bat out of hell. I just needed to get the fuck away from my family. The whole ride home was a blur. Flashbacks from the day I thought I saw my mother "killed" played in my mind.

"Can I please stay out here with you for a little while longer?"

"No, P. Momma is about to handle some business. Head home and I'll be there in a little while. Your daddy will have

a fit if he knows you out here. Go home and keep an eye on Fendi.

"He's there with Ms. Mona."

"I know, but he loves it when you play with him. Look, go ahead home, and I promise I'll bring y'all home some cake and ice cream from Baskin Robbins."

"I don't want no damn cake and ice cream."

"Watch your mouth out before I wash it out with soap! Now take your ass home!"

"I'll go ma, but I don't understand why G can't keep an eye on him."

"Listen, G, always keep an eye on you and your brother. No matter what happens in this life, both of you are supposed to look out for Fendi. He's the baby boy, and he needs his big brothers to teach him everything. I'm depending on you, Prada. Can momma depend on you?"

"Yeah, ma. You can depend on me."

"Okay! Gone head home, P! Momma loves you, and I'll be there before you know it."

"Make sure you bring chocolate cake and vanilla ice cream."

On the inside, I smiled, thinking back to that moment. She knew how to talk us into doing anything. She never had to raise her voice to get us to do what she wanted, but we also knew not to play with her. That was the last good memory I had because, in a matter of minutes, life changed. I started walking off, but I heard a car pull up and come to a screeching halt. I remember ducking behind another car and watching from a distance.

"I want my twenty grand, nigga!"

"Calm down, Chanel! Baby, I told you I was going to give it to you. A nigga needs a couple of more weeks."

"Baby, my ass! You got all these hoes out here! Put them

bitches on a stroll and get my money. Silk is going to act a fucking fool when he finds out that dope is missing. Nigga, you were supposed to turn a profit. Your ass ain't did shit. I need my fucking money, or it's lights the fuck out!"

"Stop with all them damn threats. You know I got you. This bitch is gone make sure you get that bread. Ain't that right, Mink baby?"

"That hoe better!"

"I got you, Chanel. You know I would never do anything to fuck up what we have."

After that last statement is when the first gunshot when off, I watched my mother stumble backward, holding her chest. Then another shot went off, and that's when she fell. Now that I'm thinking more about the shit, the gunshots came from inside of the car. The man leaning out the car was not the one who was shooting. I remember the pinky ring on his finger. Someone else in the car with him was the one who fired at her. I hit the steering wheel in frustration because I was trying to remember. If my coward ass hadn't run, I would have seen what they did to her.

TWO
GAVIN

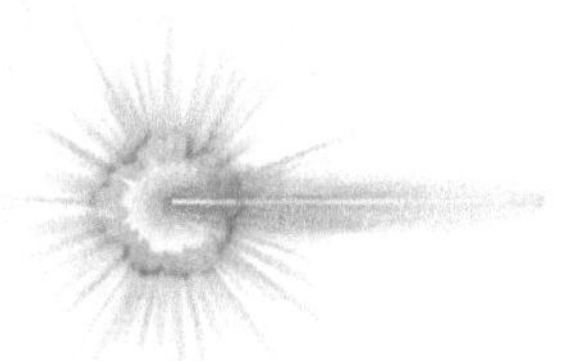

It had been a week since Prada had found his mother, and life had been so miserable for me in such a short time. It's like every week it's something different. Just knowing that my mother has something to do with what happened to Ms. Chanel scares me. Honestly, I'm scared for my sister too. Both of us have this new life with Prada and Givenchy. What if their mother doesn't like us? If that's the case, our life is going to drastically change. I probably wouldn't be so worried if Prada were handling this better. My baby is in a dark ass place, and I could do nothing about it. His family has been calling nonstop and coming over to the house. Each time they've tried, he forbids me to answer the phone or let anyone in. I needed to respect the way Prada was feeling, but at the same time, I felt like shit for not answering for them. I'm not sure how much more of this shit I can take.

"Get up, Prada!" I yelled as I pulled the covers off of him and opened the curtains in our bedroom. It was dark as fuck, and time for him to get up. All of this drunk and high shit has got to stop.

"What the fuck? Gone head on with that bullshit. A nigga got a headache!"

"That's what happens when you drink alcohol and mix it with drugs. Get up right now, Prada!"

Since he wouldn't get up, I started jumping up and down on the bed. Before I knew it, he kicked me, making my ass fall out of the bed. Without hesitation, he had me pinned to the floor with his hands wrapped around my neck.

"Prada, you're hurting me!" I managed to get out. It was as if a light switched on in his head, and he stopped.

"Fuckkkkk!" He punched a hole in the wall and rushed into the bathroom.

I sat up and pulled my knees close to me. Prada had put his hands on me, which was something he has never done. He knows this type of shit that I went through with Carlo. In my heart, I know he didn't mean to. I could see it in his eyes when he realized what he was doing. I was feeling triggered as fuck to the point where it felt like I was having an anxiety attack. I needed to get the fuck out of this house. This shit was way out of control, and I didn't know what to do. The only person that can talk some sense into him is Givenchy.

"DON'T WORRY, sis. I'm going to talk to him. Prada is in his feelings right now. When he gets like that, it's best to leave him alone until he comes down."

"He choked me this morning. I know he didn't mean too. He's just so upset about finding Chanel."

"He did what?" Miyani yelled.

"Calm down, babe. I'm going to head over to the house and talk to his ass now. That nigga knows we don't put our hands on females." G was mad as fuck. He grabbed his car keys off the table and rushed out the door.

All I could do was put my head down and cry. All of this damn drama had me emotional as fuck.

"Come on out to my she shed. We can chill out there."

I quickly wiped my face and followed her outside. Miyani was a damn kept wife for real. This nigga done had my sister a damn she shed built in the back of their house. It was the size of a damn guesthouse.

"Bitch, you so damn spoiled." I hit her on her ass as we stepped inside. The interior was dripped in gray, soft pink, and gold. It was giving me Hollywood glam vibes.

"The crazy part is that I don't even have to have all of these luxuries. As long as I have Givenchy, Gianna, and G-Baby, that's all I need. Now that's enough about me. Are you okay?" She pulled out some Stella Rosa Black and poured us both a glass.

"I'm just worried about Prada. The way he has behaved this week is out of control. I know he has a temper, but he's never displayed it with me like this. He blanked out and choked the fuck out me. In my heart, I know he didn't mean it, so I'm honestly not mad at him about that. I'm just feeling like shit is going to change. Are you aware of the seriousness of this all? Our mother has something to do with their mother being gone. What if they decide that shit is too much and leave our ass?"

"That will never happen, Gavin. Don't even think that way? Givenchy and Prada would never do that to us. Tensions are so high right now. This is a lot on them, so it's important we just fall back and let this shit play out." Miyani came over and wrapped her arms around me.

"I love you, big sis."

"I love you too. Now wipe your damn face and stop that crying. Everything is going to be okay. We just have to keep being the women we've always been to them. Flame that up and calm the fuck down." Miyani handed me the blunt, and I hogged the fuck out of it. I needed to be high to deal with this bullshit.

"Have you met her yet?"

"Nooooo! G goes to visit with the kids every day. I've yet to join them, though." I looked at her to see if I heard what the fuck she just said.

"Why doesn't he take you with them?"

"He said he'll introduce us when it's the right time. I'm cool with it. The last thing I'm about to do is be intrusive. He's getting acquainted with the mother he thought was dead. It's hard, but I can't take it personally. After all, our mother is responsible for this shit. That woman probably does not want to look at our ass anyway, and I don't blame her."

"Ole Melissa strikes again. I just can't understand why she's pure evil. Our childhood was a complete lie. The bad part about that is daddy knew and lied as well. I guess we have to wait it out."

"Yep, that's all we can do."

Miyani and I sipped wine, smoked, and chilled for hours. Our conversation was the deepest it had been in a while. Everything could be crumbling around us, but we were holding on strong to one another. In the end, it will always be us against the world.

THREE
GIVENCHY

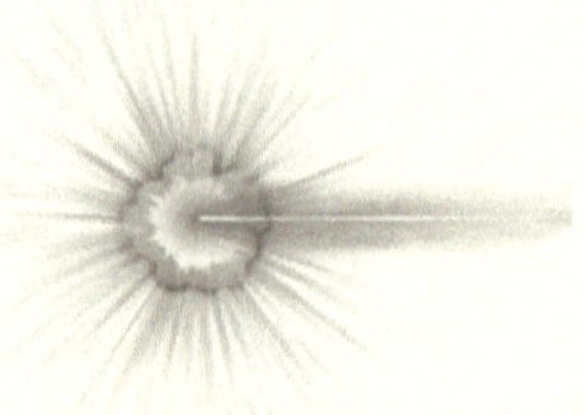

I've always thought that I could handle anything in this life. Losing my mother was a different type of hurt. At ten years old, I lost my first best friend. I worshipped the ground my mother walked on. Nobody could tell me shit about Chanel. I loved it when she would pick us up from school in her red Corvette. It was if everybody stopped what they were doing just to stare at her.

I big part of me died that day the police came to the crib and told us. Our grandma was in jail, and our father was MIA. With no other family to get us, we were placed in foster care. We never had a funeral. From behind the wall, grandma had paid a local funeral home to cremate her. When she came home, she picked the urn up, and we've had it ever since. I'm still fucked up behind that not being her actual ashes in there. Once I get shit together on the home front, I'll definitely be paying that funeral director a visit.

I just keep seeing her face in my mind. She's still one of the most beautiful women I've ever seen. Beautiful wasn't the word to describe her. All the big dope boys wanted my mother. Silk was forever in gunfights with niggas behind them trying to get her. Even as a kid, I watched how my mother played Silk ass like a fiddle. She would always throw some nigga up in his face that would make him act crazy. I've never agreed with him putting his hands on her, which wasn't easy to witness.

My mother had no problem with boxing him. However, she was still a woman, and his ass was wrong. A man should never put his hands on a woman. A bitch is a different story, so they don't count. When I say bitch, I mean Melissa and India just to name a few. Those two bitches definitely need to get their asses beat.

They will get what's coming for them in due time. Right now, I needed to focus on bringing my family together. The infamous Chanel Alexander was back in the flesh so she needed a fucking celebration of life.

"YOU JUST GONE SIT THERE and act like I'm not talking to you? This nigga Prada was pissing me the fuck off, and I was seconds away from putting hands on him.

"I told your ass I don't want to talk. Go home and

handle Miyani. Stop trying to tell me how to behave in my relationship. I'm grown as fuck, my nigga. Gavin and I are good!"

"If y'all so good why the fuck is she at my house crying? You lost your cool and put your hands on her. Since when we move like that, lil bro. Talk to me. I know you're hurt behind this shit. How do you think Fendi and I feel? We're all going through the same thing you're going through."

"That's the thing y'all not going through the same shit I'm going through. I'm mentally fucked up behind this shit. I saw her get shot, G. All I could do was run when she hit the ground. She kept telling me to leave."

"Why wouldn't you say shit?" I couldn't believe he had kept this shit to himself all of these years.

"I just put it in the back of mind. How could I come home and tell my brothers I didn't do shit to help our mother? I should have done more."

"Nigga get out your motherfucking feelings! You were a fucking kid. What the hell could you do? Just embrace the fact that our mother is alive. For so many years, we mourned her. Not many people get this chance to have their mother back. We need to throw ma dukes the biggest fucking party this city has ever seen. Hell, for Versace too. We got a fucking sister. How fucking dope is that? Get dressed. Let's go to grandma's house. It's Sunday, so you know it's about to go down." I was excited as fuck trying to cheer this nigga up.

"I'll come over later. Right now, I need to make shit right with my lady."

"That's what up. Don't put this shit off with ma. She's been asking about you the whole week. I love you, bro. For years, we yearned for her. Now that she's back, she needs to see exactly who the fuck we are. Quiet as it's kept, there's more to this story than what it appears to be. I'm just giving them time to rest up before I start asking questions.

"Why does your ass always have to start with that thinking shit?"

"Somebody's got to be the brains of this operation. I'll get up with you later, bro." We dapped it up, and I headed home.

The whole ride my mind was deep in thought about my mother and eighteen-year-old sister Versace. Obviously, she was born during the time they were being held captive. To make matters worse, Versace had recently given birth to a son. My mother let them motherfuckers escape and there has to be a good ass reason why. I'm going to get down to the bottom of it. My brothers never understand why I do the shit I do, but it's necessary. I see shit that their angry asses miss easily. That's why it's important for me to use my head with every situation. It doesn't matter how big or small it is.

"MY GOD, you are the spitting image of Silk!" my mother said as I walked in the kitchen.

Ms. Gladys and my mother were in the kitchen preparing dinner. For a second, I got lost in seeing them. My grandmother had the biggest smile. She actually looked like a weight had been lifted off her shoulders. Ms. Gladys was a tough old bird, but losing Chanel took her spirit. That spirit has found its way back to her life.

"I'm so sick of you trying to push that nigga off on us. I don't care what y'all say, that nigga ain't no damn good."

"Momma, you can't possibly hate that man after learning about everything. I've forgiven him, and you should do the same."

Before my grandma could say something, I interjected, "Every time I come here y'all arguing. After all of these years of being apart, one would think you would be all over each other."

"We've been around each other enough. I can't wait until she moves in her place Friday. She, Versace, and the baby all got to go."

"Hey, son. How have you dealt with her all of these years?" She kissed me on the cheek and walked out of the kitchen.

"How are you feeling about all of this? You haven't really voiced your opinion." Right now, I was picking her brain. I needed to know where my grandmother's head was. Knowing how she's moving makes me move with better precision.

"I've been quiet because if I say something, all hell will break loose. Now you know I missed my daughter more than anything in this world. I'm happy she's home, but the celebration is over. It's time to get down to the bottom of what the fuck has gone on. She's letting motherfuckers live who have gone against this family. Something is definitely wrong with this shit."

"I agree. Don't worry. I'm on it. I was thinking we should give ma a big party. Like she's really alive, so the streets need to know the queen is back."

"That sounds like a great idea, son. Let's make it a Team Supreme affair. The streets need to know that the price to play just went up."

"Team Supreme it is!"

"Hey, G!"

"What's good, sis? How are you and my nephew doing?"

"We're okay. Please, don't send anything else over here.

Every hour that doorbell is ringing. Fendi sent the baby and me a Rolex, Prada had a Porsche truck delivered, and you brought us a furnished home. I'm more than grateful for that. We don't need anything else. I'm just happy to have three amazing big brothers. You guys are everything mommy brags about."

"Forgive us. We've never had a sister. We're just trying to play catch up. Plus, what type of big brothers would we be if we didn't step up? I mean, you can't raise nephew alone."

"I don't have to raise him on my own. He has a father."

"It's a good thing you said that. Who is his father so that I can fuck that nigga up for getting you pregnant at eighteen, not to mention holding you hostage?"

"I can't tell you here. We have to go somewhere else to talk. Momma doesn't want me to say anything, but I have to. I know he's coming soon."

"Who is he?" She looked scared as hell all of a sudden, and I didn't like it. This only proves to me that my momma was holding back vital information.

"King Joffery."

"Wait a minute. The father of my nephew is a Haitian drug lord."

"He's my husband, G. It was an arranged marriage." She had tears in her eyes, and I grabbed her in my embrace. A nigga was heated as fuck.

"Who arranged that shit?"

"I did." my mother said as she walked inside of the bedroom. She sipped from her wine glass casually, and my anger shot the fuck up.

"We need to talk right now, not later. Let me call Prada and Fendi. We're about to get down to what the fuck has been going on all these years. You've been gone for twenty years. Shit is looking suspect all of a sudden. I need answers!"

"Last time I checked, I was the mother, and you were the child."

"Last time I laid eyes on you; I was ten years old. Back then, I was a child. I'm a thirty-year-old man who grew up without a mother. Not only that, but I'm running an empire. In case you forgot, Team Supreme is the most important thing to this family."

"Yes, I agree. Team Supreme is the most important thing to me. I'm still a part of this family. I might have been gone for twenty years, but everything I did in my absence was for Team Supreme. Call your brothers but leave your women at home!"

"Hold up! What do you mean leave our women at home? They are a part of Team Supreme, ma." One thing I don't deal well with is anyone disrespecting Miyani. She rocks a nigga's chain for a reason.

"This is a discussion that involves their mother. I'm not comfortable discussing certain shit in front of them. What you and your brothers do with them is y'all business? Until I have one-on-one conversations with them, I don't want them involved in my business. That's just that on that.

"Ma, trust me, they're good women."

"They could be the best thing God created for a man. However, in my eyes, no one is good enough for my boys. That's no disrespect to them, though. Now, call your brothers so we can discuss things."

I ran my hand over my face in frustration. This woman was doing too much. At the same time, I understood her feeling a way about Miyani and Gavin being Melissa's children. That's why I had been keeping Miyani away from her until she smooths out. It's looking like I need to have dinner with her and Miyani. I have to get the women in my life on one accord.

"See what I've had to deal with, bro?"

"Hell, she's a walk in the park compared to Ms. Gladys. Get dressed. We're having a family meeting in a little while.

"I have to go to the meeting too?"

"Absolutely! What's an empire without the princess? Don't trip. We got you. You don't have to worry about anything. We will murk anything detrimental to this family."

I kissed my lil sis on the forehead and left the room. I hit up my brothers and told them to get their ass over to the house now. Chanel Alexander had some shit going on with her, and I was ready to see what the fuck it was.

FOUR
CHANEL ALEXANDER

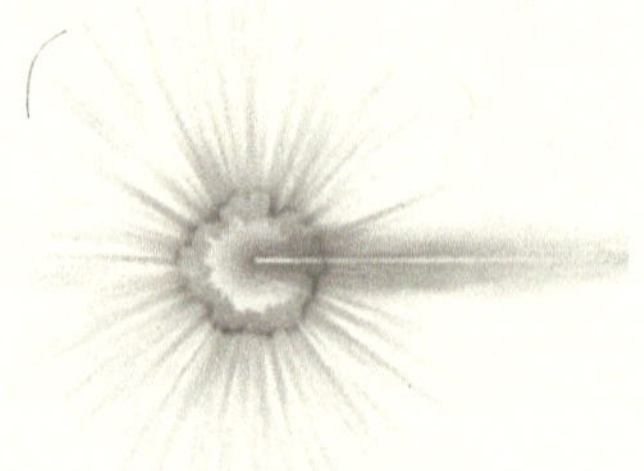

It felt good to be home with my family. For years, I waited for the day that we would be reunited. Now that I'm here, it's time to tell my story. My family may not agree with my means of survival, but they will thank me later. My boys have grown into exactly what I wanted them to be — young, rich, and ruthless as fuck. None of this shit would be possible if I didn't take one for the team. These people had better start being nicer to me, not that they haven't. From the moment I walked in the door, they've been spoiling their momma rotten. My mother, on the other hand, has been one mean ass lady. I don't know what it is, but I need to have a heart-to-heart with her. That lady was my best friend before all of this shit transpired. All I want is to make things right with my family and terrorize the motherfucking streets.

Walking in the dining room, I was shocked, looking at Silk. Why was he here? His big fine ass had been here every day since I had returned. It wasn't that I didn't want him around. It's just that his presence triggers the fuck out of me. Silk and I have some unfinished business.

I couldn't believe my family was sitting around this table dressed in all black. The iced out Team Supreme chains glistened underneath the chandelier. I inhaled deeply and took it all in. The pain I endured was not in vain. The energy in this room is one of power, wealth, and respect. Givenchy was sitting at the head of the table with his game face on. He was in full kingpin mode. I dreamed of seeing him run the fucking city. Now that it has happened, it's scary. I've been around some of the most ruthless of niggas, but none of them carried themselves like my son. After this sit-down with my family, I needed to sit down with his fiancée. She's got to be strong as fuck being with my son. His life depends on it.

"I'm sorry I kept y'all waiting. Let me get me pour myself a drink. I advise y'all to roll that shit ya smoke and pour yourself a double shot.

"It's that bad, huh?" Prada spoke angrily as he popped a pill in his mouth and chased it with Hennessy. He has always been a mean fucker. He picked that trait up from Silk's bipolar ass.

"It's only bad if you look at things one-sided," I replied.

"Well, lay the shit out there on the table. I have to get to the casino. Shit, your ass is slow dragging. Get the molasses out of your ass and tell us what the hell is going on."

Nothing has really changed about my mother. She's still a mean old ass impatient lady.

"First, I want to say that I'm so happy to be back home. There are no words to express the love you have shown Versace and me. It's like I never left."

"But you did, ma. We learned to live without you because, in our minds, you were dead. The fact that you aren't dead, had a daughter, and managed to sell her in an arranged marriage fucks me up.

My baby Fendi spoke, and, for the first time, I became emotional. He was so young when I left him. He's been silent since I returned. This was the first time since all of this happened that he's spoken a word. G being on my ass telling me to come clean is nothing. My baby boy sitting here on the verge of tears was more than enough for me to lay it out there.

"The day everything happened, I was trying to get the money back Butch owed me."

"You mean owed me. I'm still pissed about you giving that nigga my coke. None of this shit would have happened had you not been fucking that nigga Butch!" Silk yelled as he slammed his fist on the table.

"Calm down, pops. Don't raise your voice at my mother!" Givenchy spoke as if he was the damn parent.

"It's cool. He's right. I let my feelings for Butch overshadow my damn marriage. For that, I'm sorry, Silk."

"I taught your ass better than to be giving any nigga your bread. His dick wasn't that good to be giving his ass no damn coke. Hurry this shit up. I'm getting pissed off listening to this stupid shit."

"Would y'all please let her finish!" Prada yelled. All of my boys had a mean streak, and it was because of my choices.

"Melissa shot me that day when everything transpired. She shot me once in the chest and in the head. I only survived because they got me to the hospital in time — that and the fact that bullet miraculously missed vital areas of my brain. However, I was in a coma for about a month on a ventilator. My lungs collapsed several times, but they managed to save me. I learned all of this when I came to. The moment I woke up from my coma, shit got real. I woke up handcuffed to a bed in a dimly lit room where federal agents, the mayor at that time, and the governor all surrounded me.

I was immediately moved from the hospital to an undisclosed location. That alone let me know something was not right. The fucking federal government wiped me out of the system and declared me dead. I tried escaping, but each time, I was caught and beaten until I submitted. I had no idea what was going on until I was introduced to Christopher Toussaint. Basically, the United States government sold me to him."

I knocked back the shot of Cognac to calm myself down. Just reliving the first time I laid eyes on his eyes made me cringe. I hated the very sight of him.

"So, you've been in Haiti all of this time?"

"Yes. It was a part of the deal I made with the government."

"What deal?" my mother asked sternly.

"You were going to be murdered in prison. They had hired some Mexican female assassin to murder you. They allowed me to listen to conversations about the hit they were planning. Not only that they were going to separate my kids and make sure they were lost in the system, but they purposely sent you guys to that horrible foster home. The only reason you were able to get custody of them was because I made a deal with the devil. I have no regrets. To save my mother and my kids, I would do it all over again. I would rather lose out on what I love if it meant my family would prosper. That's just the type of bitch I am. It's called sacrifice. The business that we are in will always require sacrifice. Team Supreme, right?" I yelled and held my glass in the air.

"Team Supreme!" they all yelled in unison.

"The moment I agreed with them, I was placed on a private plane back to Haiti with Toussaint. When I first made it there, I immediately became one of his many women. I will not sit here and go into the details. Certain things happened to me that I don't care to discuss. It's personal, and my kids shouldn't know anything like that. Just know that my life was a living hell for the first two years in Haiti. The only thing that kept me going was the hope of getting back home to y'all.

Two years after being with Touissant, I became pregnant with Versace. What I thought was a curse became a blessing. Being pregnant with his child came with a lot of perks. You see, the government expected that man to bring me to Haiti and make my life a living hell, which he did in the beginning. That was until his coke fell off. He knew who I was from the moment they turned me over to his ass. Touissant wanted me to teach him how to cook and cut the dope himself. You see, he had other people that cooked and cut it for him. They didn't know what the fuck they were doing. He promised that if I taught him how to make his business grow, in return, he would give me a good life.

After a couple of months, his profits soared, and so did his love for me. After giving birth to Versace, he asked for my hand in marriage. Versace was his most prized possession. Anything she wanted, she could have, and because I was her mother, anything I wanted I could have as well. I solidified my spot amongst the Haitian elite while there."

"So, you've basically just been living in Haiti, not to mention living a good life? We've been here thinking that you were dead. If life was so fucking grand in Haiti, how did y'all get back here?" Prada yelled.

"Touissant was executed in a drug raid last year. Versace just happened to be at our house when it happened. We were both taken into custody immediately. The people who raided the house wore ski masks and fake police uniforms. They immediately put bags over our heads and rushed us out of the house. It wasn't until we made it to the airstrip that I realized something was off. We had the bags over our heads the whole plane ride. Once the plane landed, we were immediately thrown into the back of a van. The next thing I know, we're back here in Chicago being held in a warehouse that I later found out was where Melissa kept the bitches she trafficked. This last year has been filled with us going from city-to-city fucking around with politicians in this city. With Versace being pregnant with the baby they didn't really fuck with her too much. Which I was happy about.

Melissa and India provide women for some of the richest motherfuckers in the world. She's not some local ass Madam Mink like she was back in the day. This shit is on another level. The Melissa I knew back in the day was just a dick silly broad in my eyes. She was selling pussy for Butch and would do whatever for him. She loved that nigga but hated that he was infatuated with me. Butch thought we had something special. Little did he know, he was just a tool I used to get back at Silk but fucked myself in the end."

"Now, that you've cleared that up, explain to me why Versace has a baby by King Joffery. She's eighteen now, which means she was seventeen when she got pregnant. What the hell is she doing with that grown man?" Givenchy asked.

"Wait a minute! Who the fuck did you say her baby daddy is?" Prada asked as he banged his fists on the table.

"Hand me a Perc, bro. This shit too much," Fendi said as Prada handed him a damn pill. It's good thing I'm back because clearly my children are crazy as fuck. Then again, what did I expect? I left them with my momma, and we all know Gladys is a nut.

"That's Versace's story to tell. I've told my truths. Go ahead Versace tell your brothers how that happened."

"Really, ma?"

"Hell yeah! You have Givenchy thinking I sold your ass. Tell him the truth." Versace had the nerve to be sitting there like she was sold or some shit. She's got G looking at me as I'm some fucked up person.

"He's not some grown ass man. He's twenty-five, and I'm eighteen. I'm legal and age is nothing but a number."

"Fuck all that Aaliyah shit! Your ass still don't have no business fucking on that R. Kelly ass nigga!"

"That is not funny, Fendi. Why would you say that?"

"Yes, the fuck it is and your fast ass know it is." We all couldn't help but laugh. Versace ass didn't find anything funny.

"Anyway, I met Joffery one day when I was out with some friends. At that time, I didn't know who he was. My father kept me away from the Haiti underworld. One date turned in to me running away and living with him. For months, I stayed held up in his mansion. I became pregnant so, I had no choice but to tell my parents. The day I decided to go home is the day my father was executed, and we were brought out here. Joffery is very powerful in Haiti. He's going to come for his son."

"That nigga might be powerful in Haiti, but he's a dead man here in the Chi!" Givenchy spoke as he knocked back his shot. It was time for us to close this meeting out and move forward.

"All I can say is that I'm sorry I had to make such a crazy decision. I'm glad I did, though. You all have flourished in my absence. Everything happens for a reason. Things were meant to happen this way. Everything that has transpired brought us together in this very moment. It's time for this family to collect on all debts owed. You see, I have leverage on a lot of motherfuckers and that helps our cause. I'm all in if y'all are."

Getting all of that shit out on the table helped me breathe a sigh of relief. I told my truth, and it was time for my family to deal with and move on. We've wasted enough time letting these people breathe.

"Here you go, ma." Givenchy handed me a huge necklace box. My eyes lit up when I opened it. He had got me my own Team Supreme chain. Silk came over and helped me put it on.

"Team Supreme!" Prada yelled as he held his glass in the air.

On cue, we all stood with our glasses and did the same. It was time to shake some shit up. I hope everybody in this room understands how I'm about to morph into the bitch they hate. I couldn't do that until I cleared the air about my absence. Now it's time to hit these streets running.

FIVE
MIYANI

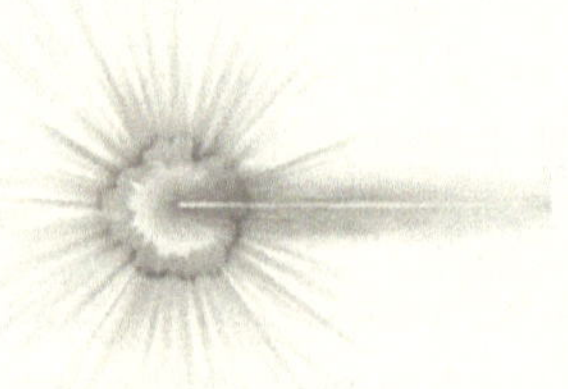

It made me happy as hell to see Givenchy so happy. Since finding out his mother is alive, he's been on a natural high. It's as if a weight has been lifted off of his shoulders. It's been well over a month since they've reunited, and we have yet to meet her. At first, I was feeling like she needs time dealing with the whole Melissa being our mother issue. Now, it's apparent that Givenchy is purposely keeping me away from his mother. Since the moment I met G, he has always made me feel incredibly important about myself as a woman. Now he got me wondering if I'm not good enough to meet his mother and sister.

I understand the whole situation with my mother. However, I'm a victim, as well. That shit has nothing to do with me. The way G was moving got me all in my feelings. My emotions are fragile, and any triggers will set me off. He's been working so hard getting ready for the opening of the Chanel House and Supreme Suites that I've been keeping the way I feel to myself. The last thing I want is for him to feel as if he has to choose between his mother and me. Plus, I don't want that man thinking I'm needy or a nagging ass woman. I would hate to run my good ass man away with this. Instead of letting my emotions get the best of me, I've immersed myself in preparing my new dance studio. It was all I really had that kept me sane. Givenchy has basically stopped me from doing all street shit.

"Good morning, son shine. Did you sleep well, mommy's baby?" I lifted my son from his crib and kissed him on the forehead. At five months old, G-Baby was huge for his age. That most likely comes from Ms. Gladys sneaking and putting baby food in his bottles. She got my baby looking like a sumo wrestler, not to mention spoiled as hell. He's such a damn crybaby that wants to be held all day.

"I'll be back in a little while. My momma and sister are moving in their cribs today. I need to get over there and make sure shit goes smoothly."

Givenchy looked so damn good in his all-black Nike jogging suit. The wheat Timbs set the whole fit off. I became lost in his aura. His energy was so magnetic. It's like when he stepped into our son's nursery, the energy elevated. This man exudes so much power. Givenchy Alexander has the type of power that scares the fuck out of a woman, but for the same reason, that very power will make her fall in love with him. This man has me completely gone over him. I honestly don't know if that's a good or bad thing.

"Is there anything you need me to do? I can go out and grab some housewarming gifts for them if you would like me to?"

"Nah! They're straight. We already got everything. That's nice of you, babe." Givenchy grabbed my chin and kissed me.

I regretted asking that pitiful ass shit. In that moment, I wanted to seize the opportunity for a chance to meet them. Come to think about it. This was the first time I heard of them moving, not that it's my business. I just find it strange that he hadn't mentioned it. I quickly walked away from him with my son.

"Miyani!"

"What?" I didn't mean to raise my voice, but I couldn't help it.

"Why the fuck are you yelling at me? You mad at a nigga or something?" He stepped in front of me, blocking my path.

"No. I'm not mad at you. I got my period. I'm just moody as fuck, that's all. Is there anything you want in particular to eat for dinner?" My ass quickly changed my tune.

"Nah! I'm straight, beautiful. I'll see you later tonight." Givenchy kissed me once more and headed out of the house.

There I was again feeling stupid and emotional. I needed to get out of this house before I lose my mind. All I've been is doing working and taking care of the household. Not tonight, I'm about to get out here with Gavin and Dream.

"I TOLD Fendi fuck him and his momma. At this point, I don't even care about meeting her."

"That's the part I don't understand. Melissa is not your mother, so what's the issue with why you haven't met her. This shit is so damn stupid to me. I told your ass them niggas were going to change now that their mother was back," Gavin stated.

"I don't think they're changing on us. It's more, so them just embracing the fact that their mother is back. At the same time, there is no reason why we shouldn't have had a sit-down with her. I mean, a sit-down is a must."

"Why don't we bring the sit-down to her? I mean, think about it. She's a fucking hood legend. You think that woman gone make her move first. She's not the type of mother that invites her sons' girlfriends over for dinner. She's the type of mother that thinks no bitch is good enough for her sons. I say we head over to her house now. Fendi sent me his location. All you hoes have to do is say the word."

Dream needed to sit her pregnant ass down. She's still in her first trimester and behaving like she's not with child. She and Fendi have been at each other throat about the shit.

"I'm down. Prada hasn't been coming home anyway so, what the fuck do I have to lose."

To hear Gavin say that shocked me. She hadn't mentioned anything to me about Prada not coming home. As a matter of fact, she had been acting like things were cool. I would definitely be making it a point to ask her about this shit later.

"I don't know if we should do that. Givenchy will be mad at me."

"So what! Prada and Fendi are going to be mad too, but

this must be done. Come on now, Miyani! You know I'm telling the truth." Of course, Dream would try to persuade me to do the shit. I swear she is such a bad fucking influence.

"I'm with Dream on this one, sis! Think about it this way. We'll be in the doghouse together." I can't believe I was about to let these hoes talk me into this shit.

"Let's go." Just like that, all of our dumb asses headed over to meet the infamous Chanel Alexander.

"LOOK AT THIS MOTHERFUCKING HOUSE, BITCH!" Dream yelled, hitting the steering wheel.

"Damn, them niggas went all out. They got her living in the biggest mansion in the subdivision." Gavin added.

"I don't know about y'all, but I'm jealous. I don't care how petty it sounds. G needs to buy me a house. I'm living in his shit."

"At least he built you a damn she shed on the property."

"Girl, I'm so tired of you talking about my she shed."

We all laughed because Gavin had been talking about it nonstop. That she shed wasn't shit compared to looking at this castle they call a house. My heart sped up, looking at G's car parked in the winding driveway. My ass was starting to have second thoughts.

"This is a lot of cars out here. I thought they were moving her in. It seems like they're having a party," Gavin added.

As we got closer, I started hearing music. We headed up to the door, and it opened before we could knock. Nettie and her girlfriend, Lexx, walked out.

"What's up, sis? What are y'all doing here?" Nettie asked. She looked surprised to see us.

"We're coming to the party! Excuse us, Nettie Boo!" Dream grinned devilishly, and we walked inside. I stopped in my tracks watching Givenchy, Prada, and Fendi stepping with Chanel. The joy on their faces spoke volumes. Those men were so happy that I really regretted coming without being invited.

"She's so pretty in person. All of those pictures they have of her do her no justice," Gavin spoke, and it was definitely true. She was living up to her name because she was draped in Chanel,

"You're right about that, Gavin. It's crazy how my daughter looks like her. I see why Ms. Gladys calls her Miss C," I heard Dream and Gavin, but I couldn't say shit.

I locked eyes with G. To see me standing there made him stop dancing. When he stopped, everybody stopped too.

"Heyyyyy, Miyani! Look, daddy, she came! You said she was too busy." My heart hurt hearing that. It confirmed my worse fear — he didn't want me to meet his mother.

"Yes, I was busy at first, but I'm not anymore." I kissed Gianna on the cheek, and that's when Ms. Gladys appeared with the rest of the kids.

"Ain't this about a bitch!" Dream spoke underneath her breath.

"We left the kids with Ms. Pauletta while we went out. These niggas actually went and picked up the kids, and not a word was said to us about it. You still think I'm over-thinking and worrying for nothing?"

"You were right, sis." I didn't have a choice but to keep it one hundred. The moment my son spotted me, he started crying. Ms. Gladys quickly handed his fat butt over. She loved my baby but couldn't deal with that crying.

"I'm glad y'all came. It's time you sit and get to know your mother-in-law." Ms. Gladys was so happy to see us there, but Chanel's face told a different story. She wasn't happy at all. She stared us up and down before walking out of the room.

"You all must be my brother's girlfriends. They've all told me about you. I'm Versace, and this is my son, Gucci. Don't worry about my momma. She's going to come around." She extended her hand, and we all shook it.

"I'm Miyani. Nice to meet you. G has told me all about you."

"I'm Gavin. He's adorable."

"Nice to meet you. I'm Dream." Once we all introduced ourselves, there was a long awkward silence.

"Come on in here. We have plenty of food and liquor in the back. This is Chanel's housewarming. I told them hard-headed grandsons of mine to let you all know about this, so don't be sitting there with them funky ass attitudes acting like y'all mad at me. Channel that energy to them niggas right there." Ms. Gladys took my baby back from me and walked off.

"Why you didn't call and let me know you were coming, beautiful?" G spoke as he walked over to where I was standing. He kissed me on the lips, but I didn't recipro-cate the loving gesture. I was mad at him.

"I didn't want to bother you while you were moving." I walked off from him. He had me fucked up thinking this shit was okay.

For the rest of the night, we chilled and ate good with the whole team. The tension was thick as fuck between them lying ass niggas and us. It was fucked up that Chanel never came back downstairs. I put both Dream and Gavin up on game with watching everything we do and say. Even though we couldn't physically see her, I felt like she was watching us. Shit felt funny. Being mad at Givenchy feels so fucked up. We never get into it or argue, besides the time he found out who my father was. Other than that, we've been cool as a fan. Not this time, though. I have every right to be mad. To pop off was something that I wasn't about to do. He knew I was pissed, and he needed to fix this shit.

BREAKFAST WAS QUIET AS FUCK. Neither of us had said a word to each other. I ended up leaving his mother's house with Dream and my sister. G stayed back to help clean, and it was daylight when he made it home, which was a first in our relationship. That man has never let the sun beat him. I don't think he was doing anything, and he had no business that I know of. At the same time, I'm not feeling the switch up. Givenchy introduced me to his dope ass vibe, and he needs to maintain it. All this new shit got me feeling some type of way.

Lately, I had been reading a lot more. Gavin has me reading *The St. Croix Cartel* by Mz. Lady P. These niggas in this book is everything. I can't wait until she drops the next part. Since I had been home more, all I loved to do was read. These hood fairytales be everything. Hell, I have my own hood fairytale right now. G is my own personal book bae, so I can definitely see why these women go crazy about these niggas.

"So, you're just gone be stubborn and not say what's on your mind?"

Looking up from my Kindle, I observed G standing up

over me. All he had on was a pair of Versace boxers with a blunt dangling from his mouth. I was eye level to his dick, which made it hard to focus on the question he had just asked.

"I don't have anything to say, Givenchy!" I got up from the bed and walked past him. He was trying to entice me at the moment. A bitch had to move around quick. My pussy has a one-track mind when it comes to G's dick. His ass knew what he was doing.

"I can't tell! You're all in your feelings about this shit with my mother. You were bold enough to show up last night, so you need to be bold enough to speak on that shit now. Stop walking while I'm talking to you. That's disrespectful, beautiful." I stopped walking and turned around to look at his ass.

"Let's be clear. I'm not in my feelings regarding your mother. It's obvious she doesn't care to meet us. That's cool with me. I don't kiss ass. Know and understand my issue is with you. You've been purposely keeping me away from your mother and sister. I would understand this shit better if you had just kept it one hundred with me. The part that hurts the most is you walking around like this shit doesn't affect me. You have no idea how this shit has Gavin and me feeling. I'm starting to believe what she says about y'all changing on us!"

"Hold on! Let me tell you something. Don't ever let what another woman feels about her man influence you to feel the same way about yours. Prada and Gavin's relationship has nothing to do with ours. We form our own opinions about what we have. We don't have the type of relationship that invites outsiders into it. I don't give a fuck if its blood. Our relationship is private and nobody's business. I'm not saying you tell our business. I'm just putting that out there. I know you're not used to fucking with a man that moves the way I do. Just understand I'm different from these niggas out here. You're about to be my wife, and I want you out here moving just like me.

If a nigga made you feel any type of way, I'm sorry. You're right, Miyani. I should have said something instead of blatantly leaving you out. I didn't do that to hurt you. I did it to protect your feelings. Prada, Fendi, and I all decided to keep y'all away until she was ready. In no way was it meant to be disrespectful. Do you accept my apology?"

"Of course, I accept your apology G. It's cool as long as you're happy and our son has a grandmother, I'm good. We're good. It's no pressure." I wrapped my arms around his neck and kissed him.

"Your happiness is more important than my own. If you're not happy, then I'm not happy. Just know that any move I make is for the greater good of you. I will never let anyone hurt you, Miyani. I love your beautiful ass!"

"I love you too."

"I just have to know this one thing. Were y'all really trying to have a sit-down with OG Chanel?" He laughed, but I didn't see shit funny. We were on a mission that failed miserably.

"Hell yeah!"

"Good move. She's very impressed and wants you to come to the house today. Get dressed so that I can drop you off. Make sure you dress to impress and rock your chain. Let her know who the fuck you are!" He grabbed two handfuls of my ass and kissed me passionately.

Just hearing that Chanel wanted me to come over the house had me nervous. Hell, for all I know, she could be calling me over there to murder my ass. After getting dressed, I made sure to throw my gun in my all-black Birkin bag. I have to be prepared for whatever. It's a damn shame Melissa put us in this fucked up situation. Come to think of it I need to make sure I keep this shit on me at all times.

"GO IN THERE and be exactly who you are, beautiful. There's no need to do too much and don't do too little. This is one of those times where what I say to you really matters. Look at me, Miyani! You have to go in there with your chin?"

"Up."

"And what else?"

"My chest the fuck out!" I yelled with so much passion.

"That's right, baby! Talk to me dirty. That shit makes my dick hard!"

The whole ride over to Chanel's house G gave me a pep talk. He really had me feeling myself. My man had me feeling like I could take over the world. If your nigga at home doesn't hype you up like this, leave his ass.

Givenchy and I walked inside of his mother's house hand in hand. His mother was sitting in her beautiful pink and black office. She was sitting back in a chair shaped like a throne.

"Have a seat, Miyani. Bye, Givenchy!"

"Damn! It's like that?"

"Yes, it is. We don't need a mediator. Do we?"

"No, ma'am, we don't need a mediator."

"I'm out of here. You girls play nice now." Givenchy lifted my chin and slipped his tongue in my mouth like his mother wasn't in this room.

Once G left the room, there was silence in the office as I

sat across from her. I'm glad I was high and calm. Her stare was so intimidating, but I didn't break. I stared right back at her.

"I just want to say that I'm so sorry for everything that my mother did to you."

"You don't have to apologize for her bullshit. Let's get something straight! I didn't request us to sit down to blame you for anything. That bitch Melissa was fucked up before you or your sister was a thought. This is about your intentions with my Givenchy.

My son lets me know he's in love by the way he brags and goes hard for you. I can see that you're in love with him, as well. You're sitting across from me, rocking not only his chain but also his ring. Did he tell you the history behind that ring?"

"Yes, he did."

"Great, so I don't have to go into detail about the importance of it. I knew that one day my sons would end up with women. I just never anticipated they would fall in love with the daughters of my enemy. It's not an issue with me anymore. I'm just concerned about where your loyalty lies. I need to know that you stand ten toes down behind Team Supreme!"

"I'm ten toes for Givenchy! My baby takes Team Supreme seriously. I know how much he loves this family. Loyalty is the most important thing to him. That man doesn't ever have to test my loyalty because it lies with him. Ms. Chanel, I love your son. From the moment he came into my life, he has shown me what real love is. He's given me a family and shown how a family is supposed to be. My entire life has been a lie, and Melissa is the cause of it. I don't give a fuck what happens to her. To be honest with you, she's already dead in my eyes. I'm Team Supreme until the death of me." I took a sip of my champagne and sat back in the seat. She lit a Newport and handed me a file.

"That's good to hear. Check that out." I took the folder, and it was pictures of India and her attorney.

"I can't believe she's so invested in trying to get Gianna back." All I could do was shake my head as I thumbed through the pictures and documents.

"What I can't believe is this she's still living? She was supposed to be dead the moment that rat made an appearance!"

"Givenchy said he had it handled." I took a long sip from the champagne flute she handed me. Lord, I had a feeling this conversation was about to go left.

"Sometimes, we have to take matters into our own hands for the people we love. You see, Givenchy likes to strategize, which is the greatest part of him. It keeps him ahead of the game. That's why this family has flourished. Givenchy doesn't like to use force until his hand is forced to do so. That's why we have to handle some shit on our own. We'll call it being proactive?"

"The car is ready, ma'am."

"Thank you, Rallo. We will be right out." This lady had a damn driver. Rallo wasn't bad looking either. I wonder did her psycho sons know about this man.

Chanel stood to her feet and put her cigarette out.

"Where are we going, Chanel?"

"We are going to be proactive, daughter."

Part of me felt like I should call G. The other part knew that Chanel was right. This shit needed to be handled. Never in a million years did I think I would be involved in shit like this. All I've ever wanted to do was dance, and now I barely find the time. I can't help but feel like I'm losing the best part of me. I immediately shook the thought out of my mind. Right now, I needed to focus. *Givenchy was going to kick my ass!* I thought to myself.

TWO HOURS **Later**

"Welcome to Barnaby and Bennett Associates! How can I help you?" Chanel and I had walked into the law firm where India's attorney was a partner.

"We're here to see Andrea Barnaby."

"She's not seeing any clients today."

"She's expecting us." Before the receptionist could say anything else, Chanel and I were already down the damn hall of the firm opening doors.

"Wait a minute! You can't go back there!" The receptionist tried to grab me, but I quickly turned around and punched her ass.

"Get the fuck back!"

"I think you broke my nose!" Blood was pouring from her nose.

"If you put your hands on me again, I'm going to break your fucking neck!"

"What is the meaning of all this? Who are you? Oh my god! What happened to you? I'm about to call the police. She rushed past us and over to the receptionist. To hear her ass speak about calling the police had me a little shook.

"Andrea, you need to listen to me and listen to me good. If you mention anything about the police again, I'm going to put a bullet in your head," Chanel calmly spoke while tapping her gun against her temple.

"Please don't hurt us! What do y'all want?"

"Where is India hiding out?" She asked.

"Who is India? I have no idea who India." The bitch

was flat out lying, and that angered me. I'm not sure what came over me. Without hesitation, I hit the bitch across the face with my gun.

"Stop fucking playing with us! Where the fuck is India laying her head at?" I asked in a calm but stern voice.

"Bitch, you lying to me! Don't play with my fucking intelligence. I know that you're her adoptive mother, so if anybody knows where India is, your ass does. Your stupid ass is out here trying to help her take my granddaughter, and she's on a crime spree with her birth mother. India is not thinking about your ass bitch. All she wants is Gianna. You're expendable to her, and you know it. Where the fuck is that bitch at? Before you answer, I want you to think very carefully about the answer. Look at this picture. Maybe that will jog your memory."

"Noooo! Please don't hurt them. I promise to tell you whatever you want to know. Let's sit down and I'll you everything." She was clearly shook the fuck up. After whatever Chanel showed her on that phone, it made her change her tune quick.

"That a girl. Where is India hiding at?"

"She's gone back underground. They pulled her off the case they were building against Melissa Mills. They had no idea that she was her birth mother. I told her a long time ago to tell Givenchy the truth, but she never did. She wasn't here to hurt y'all family. She was on a damn case to take Madam Mink down but being back made her miss Gianna and Givenchy. So, she out of the blue, she said quit, knowing that's not how the shit works. I'm sorry only the higher up know where she is. Please don't hurt my other daughters. They have nothing to do with this. I'll pay you whatever you want, but please don't hurt them!" Andrea was pleading for dear life. The way was she acting led me to believe that she was telling the truth.

"So, she was still working undercover?" I asked.

"Yes! The only reason she came back was to take down Melissa Mills. She had no idea it would send her right back to a life she regretted giving up."

"If she reaches back out to you, tell that hoe she is no longer welcome on the streets of Chicago. Police bitch or not. She's a dead woman for playing with my family. Make sure this visit stays between us. I know where you lay your head, and I make home visits too. Don't fuck with me."

As we walked out of the office, she placed a small snow globe on the receptionist's desk.

"So, what do we do now?" I asked as we walked outside to Chanel's awaiting car.

"We wait for India to show up. Let's go shopping."

As we drove away, there was a loud explosion that caused the car to shake. Looking through the back window, I realized that the damn attorney office had just exploded. Chanel didn't flinch. She just simply put her shades on. Here it was I thought I was going to have a conversation with Chanel. I had no idea it would turn into a damn murder scene. Having a mother-in-law is about to be an adventure for sure. I can only imagine what she has in store for her first meetings with Gavin and Dream.

SIX

DREAM

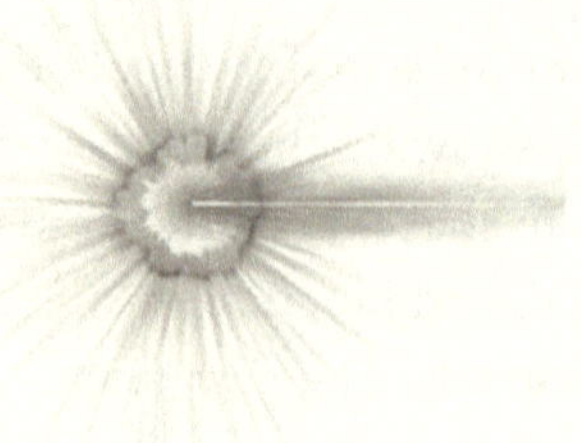

"You can have a piece of my love,
It's waiting for you..."

FENDI and I sang "Piece of my Love" by Guy as we cruised down Lake Shore Drive. Today was the first day that we've been able to spend an entire day to ourselves. He had been so wrapped up in getting shit straight for Chanel that we hadn't had time. This shit affected him greatly, and I sympathized with him. That's one of the main reasons I've let the shit go about meeting her. My mouth slick as fuck, so I'll fuck around and curse her the fuck out. That would make Fendi want to beat my ass. The last thing I ever want to do is disrespect this man's mother again. Last time I disrespected her, he damn near killed my ass. I don't have time to be beefing with my man behind his crazy ass momma. When she's ready to meet me, she will reach out.

It felt good to be in such a good place with Fendi. Ever since he found out I was pregnant; he's been so happy. He just knows I'm having a boy. I'm three months pregnant and ready for this shit to be over already. As we drove, Fendi kept his hand on my thigh. I don't know about other women, but it's small shit like this that be feeling so damn good. I've had my fair share of men that I personally liked, but none of them are like Fendi. They don't even compare. If someone had told me that I would end up with this nigga, I would have told them to stop lying. Never did I think I would find so much happiness after years of being unhappy.

Fendi pulled up to one of his rental properties, and I instantly got an attitude. I thought we were spending time together, not working.

"Fix your face. This won't be long. I'll be right back out, babe. I just need to run in here and grab these rent payments." Fendi hopped out of the car at a rental property before I could say anything to him. He knew to hurry his ass up too.

I distinctly told him we weren't working today. All I wanted to do was spend some time with my man. Right about now, I wished I could smoke me a damn blunt. He didn't have me working on this particular property. The shit was ghetto as fuck. A group of women was sitting outside drinking and smoking. He needs to stop their ass from doing that shit. It brings the property value down. The way them hoes were mind fucking my man made me want to get out and fight.

This was why his ass didn't want me over this property. It's a building full of hoes over here. Knowing Fendi's slick dick ass, he had probably fucked some of these Section 8 bitches. A short time later, Fendi emerged and got back in the car.

"Why you let them sit out here like that? They look like ghetto birds. The shit brings the property value down."

"They cool. This is the hood Dream. This is what people do. They chill in front of their homes. As long as they don't get to fighting and making shit hot, I'm cool with it."

"That's the problem. You're a little too cool with it. You need to put that one on my roster and let me clean that shit up. You're slacking, Fendi." He hit the steering wheel hard as hell.

"Let's be clear, Dream! This is my shit. Before I met you, I was running my own shit. Yes, you help to elevate the fuck out my properties but watch the disrespect. Lately, you be trying to talk to me as if I'm your son. I'm a grown ass man, so don't try to son me. I'm the one with a big dick, not you. Stop telling me I'm slacking. You're starting to piss me the fuck off."

I was looking at this nigga like he had lost his mind. Part of me wanted to go in on his ass, but I left it alone. That was also my cue to stay the fuck out of his business. Fendi was one of those niggas that don't like to listen, so you got to stop talking to him and let him fall on his ass.

"Why are you heading back toward the house? I thought we were going to eat?"

"I got some shit I need to handle."

This nigga was lying. It was cool, though. I wasn't about

to kiss his ass. He could drop me off at this point. I wanted to swing on his ass, so I needed to get out of the car. For the rest of the ride to the house, I was quiet. The nigga had an attitude all of a sudden, and I didn't want to be around his ass.

Today was one of those days I regretted being pregnant. My ass would be getting in my car and going to get fucked up. I was quickly reminded of one of the very reasons I never really had been in a relationship. Niggas be having mood swings like bitches. Fendi's far from a bitch, so I'm lost as to why he's all in his feelings. It's cool, though. I'll never weigh in on any of his business again.

IT WAS SUNDAY, and the whole family was going over to Ms. Gladys as usual. I really wasn't feeling like going, so I decided to sit this one out. I'll be mad later when I'm hungry, but not now. I'm not feeling sitting at the table with Chanel. She's basically given us her ass to kiss. Although she had met up with Miyani, she still hadn't reached out to Gavin and me, which was cool. I feel no type of way. As far as I'm concerned, we never have to form a relationship. She loves my daughter, and that's enough for me. I've never been the type of bitch to kiss a nigga's family ass, and I'm not about to start now.

"Why you still lying around?" Fendi asked as he snatched the covers off me.

"I'm not going?"

"Yes, the fuck you are. My mother is going to be there, and she told me to make sure you come. So, get the fuck up!"

"I'm not going, Fendi. I understand your mother may

want me to come, but she also could have called me herself. The last time she saw me, she gave me her ass to kiss. As far as I'm concerned, it is what it is."

I yanked the covers back from his ass and closed my eyes. This nigga thought telling me that would make me jump up and be excited to go. I'm good. Chanel shitted on us in a room full of people, and them niggas stood there and let the shit happen. This Team Supreme shit is getting to be too much. I didn't sign up for all this extra shit.

"Let's get something straight! My mother is not one of these bitches in the streets, so don't handle her like she a nobody. She's my fucking mother with your tough ass! You're the mother of my kids and my soon to be wife! Why the fuck wouldn't you want to come if she invited you? You gone have to get off that childish shit if we're taking this shit to another level. I'm not marrying nobody that thrives off of petty shit!"

I quickly jumped out of bed and got up in his face.

"You don't have to marry me at all!" I snatched the ring off my finger and launched that bitch across the room. Fendi Alexander had me fucked up.

"You lucky it's the Lord's day because I would beat your ass for that! On my daughter, I'm not giving this bitch back, ungrateful ass bitch!"

"If I'm a bitch, your momma's a bitch!" I couldn't stop myself from saying it if I wanted to.

I immediately regretted saying it. Honestly, I went too far. Fendi yoked me up by my shirt and slammed me into the wall. He wanted to hit me, but he didn't. Instead, he kissed me on the lips and walked out without another word.

I wanted to go after him but knew that I shouldn't. Although, I was mad at the way he was talking to me. I shouldn't have called his momma a bitch, even though she is a bitch for the way she had been acting toward us.

I hadn't had many sad days since I met Fendi, but this may be the hardest ever. I had no clue why this nigga was popping off on me so hard. It was like one minute we were cool, and the next, we're about to kill each other. I'm not used to all of these emotions. I think these pregnancy hormones were making the shit worse. Any other time, I want to fight with his ass. Lowkey, my feelings were hurt as fuck. I understand he loves his momma. At the same time, it's not right for him to disregard my feelings to please her. He needed to stand up for my respect as well.

My daughter was already with Ms. Gladys, so I laid back down. Fendi was on his way over there, so he could get her. I'm sticking to my guns and not going to Sunday dinner. I'll just have to deal with Fendi later.

AFTER WAKING up from my nap, I checked my phone. I had so many missed calls and messages saying come to the hospital Fendi had been shot. The room started to spin out of control, and I begin to breathe erratically. The pounding on my door helped me to focus. I quickly jumped from my bed and raced to answer. Without checking to see who it was, I yanked the door open.

"Why haven't you been answering? We've been calling your ass like crazy! You got everybody panicking Dream!" G yelled.

"I'm sorry. I've been asleep. My ringer was off, and I didn't know. Where is Fendi? What happened?"

"He got hit up sitting at a red light. Get dressed and come outside."

"Where's my daughter? Is she okay?"

"Just get dressed, sis. We have to go." Prada tried to reach out and grab me, but I pushed his hand away.

"No! I'm not going anywhere until y'all tell me what's going on." My heart was racing. Something was wrong.

"She was in the car with him. A bullet grazed her, but she's fine. Fendi dived on top of her and saved her life. Right now, he's not doing too good. Please get dressed so that we can get to the hospital." G's eyes became glossy, and I could have sworn I saw that nigga shed tears. Yeah, shit was real. G never shows emotions.

As I got dressed, I begged God to save my man. We couldn't end before we ever got a chance to really begin. Heaven needed to wait because my kids and I needed more time. I was so mad at myself for not going to Sunday dinner. I didn't have to be petty. Ms. Charlotte always used to tell me my stubborn ways would fuck me up one day. Today is that day I thought would never happen.

We rode to the hospital in complete silence. I was in a complete daze. I was there physically, but mentally I was a million miles away.

About twenty minutes later, we made it to the hospital. The family room was filled to capacity. Looking at Miyani and Gavin crying let me know things weren't looking good. They looked at me sympathetically, and that shit broke me. Chanel was sitting stone-faced. Everybody else was sad and showing their emotions, not her, though. Her face held no emotion.

"There's no time for all that crying. Wipe your face and get ready to talk to these doctors. I'm lost as to why y'all crying like my baby is dead or something!" Ms. Gladys snapped. Seconds later, a doctor came in, and Ms. Gladys gripped my hand tight.

"Good evening, I'm Dr. Ahamad. I performed the surgery on Mr. Alexander. He is out of surgery and in recovery as of right now. When he came in here, he didn't look good at all. We actually lost him during the surgery, but he's a fighter. He has to have a guardian angel because he was hit about ten times. Right now, he's on a ventilator in a medically induced coma so his body could heal. It's still touch and go. Our biggest concern is internal bleeding. If he can make it through these next couple of days, he'll be just fine.

Just hearing this shit hurt. I just wanted to hear his voice, even if it was cursing me out.

"What about my daughter?"

"She's just fine. Nurse Neal will take you back to where she is. You can come back and visit with Mr. Alexander first thing in the morning. You all can go home and get some rest."

"Yo, Doc! Let me holla at you for a minute," G voiced to the doctor while he and Prada followed the doctor out of the room.

"I'm not leaving this hospital. Miyani, take my baby home with you, please."

"Okay, sis. You know we got you." I hugged both her and Gavin.

"Thank you, Jesus!" Ms. Gladys spoke as she exhaled. She wrapped her hands around me, and we hugged for a good minute.

"Y'all go ahead and get them babies' home. Momma! Let Versace and the baby go home with you. I'm going to stay with my son."

"Hell, nah! Versace's got her own damn house. Why the hell she got to come back to my house? Hell, to the mother-fucking no! Her and that hollering ass baby can keep up all that noise where they pay the bills at." Ms. Gladys doesn't give a fuck what she says out of her mouth. She rushed out of the family room before anyone could say anything.

"Versace and the baby can come to my house. I don't mind. Hell, CJ and I could use the company. It ain't like Prada's coming home anyway."

"I'll check on you in a little while. Don't let my momma get to you," Versace whispered in my ear.

Everybody was gone now, and I was by myself. I took that as my opportunity to cry. In that moment, I could just be human and get all of my emotions. Lord knows this family made it hurt for a bitch to be emotional. That added with not wanting Chanel to see me in tears. She was really checking me out to see if I was worthy of her son. Little did she know, I was the best motherfucking that ever happened to her son. Hopefully, we can create an understanding so that Fendi will wake up and see us in a better place. In the meantime, I had to put my game face on. She's thinking I'm playing checkers, but really, I'm a chess master.

***

"THANKS FOR KEEPING her for me this week?"

"Girl shut the fuck up! That's my god baby, and we're family. Right now, we all have to stick together. Lord knows everything is falling apart. It's been so hard trying to get a minute with Givenchy. He, Prada, Gunna, Butta, and Nettie have been hitting the streets like crazy trying to see who behind the shit."

"Fendi need to wake his ass up!"

I stood from my seat and walked over to the bed he was in. He was still in a coma. The day after his surgery, Fendi had to be rushed back up to surgery because blood clots had formed and needed to be removed. They were literally saying he might not make it. That shit was so scary. Now, I'm just ready for him to wake up. It's been a week since I heard his voice, and it's driving me crazy.

I grabbed some wet wipes and began to clean his face at the same time his nurse came in.

"Visiting hours are over!"

"Nah, she's good. This is his sister-in-law."

"She knows who I am. Remember when I told you about the bitch that wasted that drink on my dress that time? Well, this is her ass."

"You don't have to talk like I'm not in the room. I'm Niara Neal, and yes, I did waste some shit on your dress. So what! you should never have been fucking my man."

"Oh, hell no! Don't think we won't drag your ass in this hospital! Don't play with my bitch behind her nigga. That's some shit we don't do. Get the fuck out of here and go give out some meds. Make sure you take some too because clearly, your ass is unbalanced."

She had me hot coming in my baby's room on this bull-shit — no wonder she had been kissing Chanel ass and going out of her way for the family.

"She ain't got to go. A bitter bitch never bothers me. I'm secure as fuck when it comes to Givenchy Alexander. That's my man. I got that nigga's heart and soul, not to mention his firstborn son. Let's be clear. While you're going around throwing out fraudulent accusations, you were never his woman. Beloved, you were a side bitch that wanted a main bitch's position. Your coward ass pulled that stunt at a kid's party. That alone lets me know that you're a weak ass bitch. That was the only pass you get. I guarantee you I'm beating your ass if you think about playing with me."

"Periodtt!" I had to chime in and say something.

Miyani had turned gangster bitch overnight, and I loved that shit. It felt good seeing her stand up for herself. She's never been scary. Miyani let's shit build until she can't take it anymore. I've always told her to let people know off top not to fuck with her. Givenchy has changed everything about Miyani. I love the way he pours into her. He makes her feel pretty, worthy, and appreciated. I'm so damn happy for my friend. She was living a hood fairytale out of this world. After the shit my girl has been through, she needs this type of love.

"Like I said, she needs to leave before I call security!" She laughed and walked out of the door.

"Oh, hell no!"

"Let her go I'm not about to go back and forth with that hoe. She big mad that nigga's love me. Fuck her. I have to get out of here, anyway. Don't worry, sis. He'll wake up soon," Miyani spoke as we exchanged hugs before she left out.

Turning back around to focus on Fendi, I felt the urge to climb in be with him. I couldn't, though, due to all the tubes. Instead, I grabbed my throw blanket and climbed in the reclining chair next to his bed.

"Well, baby. It's just you and me now." I kissed Fendi on the forehead and held his hand until I fell asleep.

"YOU DID ALL OF THIS YOURSELF?" Chanel asked as she walked around Club Bliss. This was her first time being there. We had to stop here before heading over to the hospital. Although we had been in the hospital together, we didn't really talk. Our only conversation was about Fendi's care. I was grateful that she wasn't acting like a bitch to me. My ass wasn't in the right place mentally to deal with it. My man wasn't waking up, I'm pregnant, and I haven't seen my daughter. Everything was just all too much for me at the moment. Nonetheless, I was handling this shit like a boss. Fendi would be proud of me.

"Yes, he left me in charge of his businesses when he was locked up, and I managed to turn them all around."

"He told me that you're extremely good with numbers. All he did was brag about his thieving baby Dream." I instantly became embarrassed. Why would his messy ass tell his momma about me stealing from him? No wonder she was acting funny with my ass.

"I can't believe he told you that."

"Don't worry, Dream. I don't hold anything against you. From the moment I came back, my boys have bragged about these women that they love so much. I've had to be the judge of that myself. I've been out of the loop for years. Now that I'm back, I want to make sure everybody who's part of this family is who the fuck they say they are, not to mention capable of handling what comes with it."

"So, what are your thoughts about Fendi and I being together?" I just needed to know what she thought. Honestly, it wouldn't change my feelings for him. A bitch needed to know so that I could move accordingly.

"You and Fendi are perfect. Two crazy people belong together."

"I am not crazy, Ms. Chanel."

"Dream, you, my dear, are crazy than a motherfucker. Any woman that robs a man of his shit and comes back a year later to give it back is a nut, not to mention you introduced him to the baby he didn't know he had. Not only are you crazy, but your ass is brave. A brave bitch is exactly what Fendi needs. Come on. We need to meet with my mother on the west side. I wanted to tell her I needed to get back to the hospital in case Fendi wakes up. Instead, I headed out with her and her driver. There was no telling the shit Chanel and Ms. Gladys were about to put me in.

SEVEN

MS. GLADYS

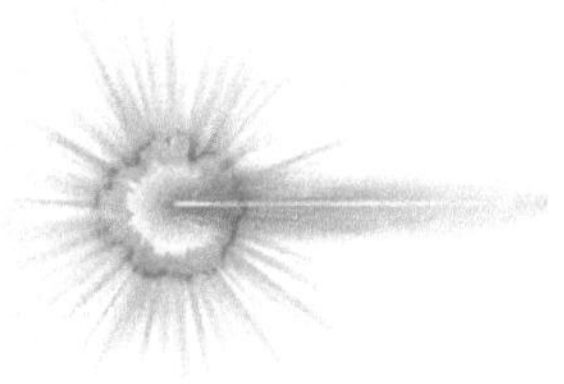

From the moment I found out my daughter Chanel was alive, I've been livid. So much shit was replaying in my mind from the past. Just knowing motherfuckers had crossed me brought me completely out of retirement. That added with the fact that a motherfucker thought it was okay to make an attempt on my grandbaby's life. All bets are off at this point. It was about time this family took out every fucking body that trespassed against us.

The problem with that is so many people wanted us gone. These motherfuckers want the table I built. I'll die and go to hell before I let that happen. It was imperative I get out and handle some shit that had been long overdue.

"Ms. Gladys, are you sure about this?" Butta asked.

"I'm positive. This motherfucker took my money and lied to me. There go Chanel right there." Butta and I quickly got out of the car.

"Why the hell does she got Dream with her?"

"You know Chanel is giving them girls hell behind them boys of hers. I taught Miyani, Dream, and Gavin well. They can handle themselves just fine. Chanel loves them girls, but she's lowkey toughing them up. It's crazy how she just came back and jumped right back into things."

Chanel may have her sons fooled but not her momma. The version she gave us was the clean one, but I'm waiting to hear the uncut version.

"Yeah, Ms. Chanel is something serious."

"Go around back and cut the security feed. Then stand out here and make sure no one comes in."

Butta jogged around back, and I walked across the street where they were.

"Why are we at a damn funeral home, old lady?" Chanel asked.

"Oh no! Funeral homes give me the creeps. It's like they have all these damn doors. You make a mistake and walk in, then boom a dead body! I'm good. I'll wait for y'all to come back out."

"Dream, bring your scary ass on!" We laughed as I basically dragged her ass inside.

"Welcome to Woodlawn Chapel? How can I help you all?"

"I'm looking for Mr. George. Is he available?"

"He's in a meeting with a bereaved family. Are you here to make arrangements?"

"Yes! Tell him Gladys Alexander is here to collect!"

"Ma!"

"Oh Lord! Dream added.

"I'm not sure I understand, Ms. Alexander."

"Just tell him to wrap that shit up. We'll wait."

"What the hell going on?" Chanel asked under her breath as I sat next to her on the sofa.

"I paid this man ten thousand dollars to pick up your body from the coroner and cremate you. He was also instructed to save some of your ashes and put it inside of our family vault. That way, when we all go, we would be together. You are very much alive, which means he took my money and never got your body from the hospital. I need to know who is behind that. I've cried over an urn for years that didn't hold your remains. This motherfucker is going to tell me something. I winked my eye at the receptionist as I waited patiently.

About ten minutes later, he finally brought his old ass back out, and the family that was making arrangements walked out of the funeral home.

"Dream stand by the door and make sure the receptionist doesn't leave. If she blinks wrong, kill her ass! Where the fuck is my money?" I took my switchblade out on his old ass.

"Wait a minute now! This is my granddaughter! What is this meaning of this, Gladys?"

"Sit your old ass down. My momma asked you a question." Chanel had her gun pointed in the middle of his forehead. He quickly sat down on the couch.

"You heard who she said she was? That's my daughter Chanel." I pulled my Black & Mild from my purse and flamed it up. I waited for it to register in his head just what the fuck I was getting at.

"Now wait a minute, Gladys! I did what you told me to do."

"I'm going to ask you one time and one time only. Who paid you to cover the shit up?"

"I'm sorry, Gladys. It was out of my control. Commander Burke showed up along with Madam Mink. I had no choice but to do as they said. He said that he would shut me and all my locations down. Madam Mink threatened to expose me for having sex with her girls. They had pictures of me. I couldn't afford for my wife to know about that. I'm sorry. My hands were tied."

"Ahhhhhhhh!" He hollered in pain as I sliced his ear off.

"Go get my ten thousand dollars!"

"W-w-what? I don't have that type of money." I laughed out because he really thought I didn't know what the fuck is going on.

"You think I forgot that you wash Madam Mink's money through here! Take me to the casket room!"

"Just do it, grandad! Give them the money," the receptionist cried and pleaded.

"I advise you to listen to her," Chanel said.

Reluctantly and writhing in pain, he slowly took us to the casket room. One by one, he opened wall panels behind the sample caskets. Each one held stacks of money and bags of pills.

"You don't understand that's not Madam Mink's cash. That's Mr. Butch's money!"

"Oh, really. Well, tell Mr. Butch Chanel took his shit!" She smacked him across the head with the gun.

I only came in here trying to get information and my damn money. Hell, I got that and way more than I expected.

For the next couple of hours, we held him and his

granddaughter at gunpoint. It was so much money we had to call Givenchy, Prada, Butta, Nettie, and Gunna to help pack the cash up. Of course, Givenchy and Prada went on and on about being left out of the loop. I didn't have time for all that negativity in my life. We got word that Fendi had woken up. Today was an excellent motherfucking day for Team Supreme.

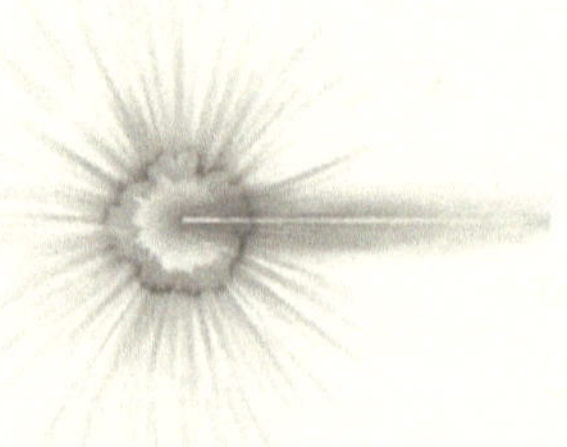

EIGHT

FENDI

The more I laid in bed, the angrier I became. A nigga needed to hurry up and heal. I just keep reliving the night I was hit up. Those punk ass pigs tried to assassinate me while I had my daughter in the car. Shit is about to get real as fuck across the city. Apparently, every motherfucker in the city was against Team Supreme. If they want a war, that's exactly what the fuck they're going to get. I'm fucked up behind these niggas thinking it was cool to pull this shit while my daughter with me. I have to get my lick back!

"You need to stop smoking, Fendi. Your ass is never

going to heal getting high!" Dream was fussing as usual. She was another reason why I was ready to get well. I couldn't do shit without her nagging a nigga. A nigga had been down for too long. I was finding it hard to deal with not being able to do anything.

"I told you this shit helps me sleep through this fucking pain!"

"Take these Tylenol 3's. It should help." Dream tried to hand me two pills, but I knocked them out of her hand.

"Fuck this shit! I give up." Dream walked out of the room and made sure to slam the door behind her.

I told her ass to stop giving me all them damn pills. That shit is not helping. Plus, I don't want to become dependent on them like Prada. Having one pill head in this family is enough. Even though the nigga swear he got the shit under control, he doesn't. I love my brother, but I would rather fight my demons with these trees.

"Why are you giving my girl such a hard time?" Miyani said as she busted in the room.

"I'm not trying to give her a hard time. On some real shit, sis, a nigga is frustrated. I'm just ready to get the hell out of this bed. Fuck niggas tried to kill me while I had my daughter. I've got to get out of this fucking house and on the streets to get at them niggas."

It's like none of the women in this family understood a nigga had shit to do. Plus, I'm known in the streets for laying niggas down. These bitch ass niggas may think I'm soft letting a nigga get up on me.

"Well, you might as well cut the bullshit out. Your ass almost died, and you just woke up. It will be a minute before you can get your ass up out of that bed. Your hard-headed ass needs to heal completely before thinking you can be out in the streets on some revenge type shit."

Miyani was walking around the room cussing and putting me in my place. My brother done turned this damn ballerina out. She used to be quiet as a church mouse, but now she is barking orders. She and Dream needed to leave a nigga alone.

"Here you go!"

"Yes! Here I go. You are all Dream has Fendi. She doesn't have parents, siblings, cousins, or any of that shit real families have. Outside of you and Miss C, she's alone. Dream is hardcore and talks shit because it helped her survive. I'm not sure if you guys talk about her early years of being in foster care, but she was treated horribly. Dream has this really tough exterior because all of her life, she's had to protect herself. On the inside, she's nothing but a scared little girl. Take it easy on my dawg. She's been so fucked up dealing with what happened to you. Being pregnant with your child is not helping. She's emotional. She's going to kill me for telling you this, but she's out there on the verge of tears. Stop yelling at my girl and let her take care of you properly."

It would take Miyani to bring her ass in here and set me straight. If I wouldn't have to fight my big bro, I would cuss her ass out too, but she was right.

"This shit got me fucked up, sis! Them niggas got down on me while I had my daughter. I got to get right and fuck them niggas over!"

"Well, get healed up so you can do that. Plus, you know your crazy ass family is wreaking havoc on the city. You made G cry. Make sure you don't tell him. He'll kill me." She laughed and walked out of the room. Miyani's ass should never have told me that. I'm definitely going to clown his bitch ass for crying.

Just thinking about what my family going through

behind this shit makes a nigga mad as fuck. I got to heal so I can make niggas' families suffer just like mine. The only difference is that they'll be sitting on the front pews of the church mourning. When I hit, I don't miss. I flamed up another blunt. It was the only thing that kept me calm and helped me sleep through the pain.

Dream thought I just wanted to get high, but it was the only thing that helped. This shit had me all fucked up.

"Da-Da!" My daughter had pushed the door open and waddled in. Just seeing her smiling made a nigga's heart go soft.

The love I receive from her and Dream is something a nigga can't describe. Before they came into my life, I lived the bachelor's life to the fullest. Now, I can't wait to get home to them. One minute I had no kids, and now I have a daughter and one on the way. Outside of all the bullshit that's going on, life is great for a nigga. Getting money used to be my main priority, but now my main priority is the family I've created.

"Hey, daddy baby!"

"Up Up!" She started to cry, and it frustrated me because I couldn't pick her up.

"I'm sorry, baby. Daddy can't pick you up right now. My daughter was screaming, and it was fucking me up. She had fallen out in the middle of the floor, throwing a temper tantrum.

"Yo, Dream!" I was trying my best to yell, but I couldn't the shit hurt like hell. As bad as I hated to admit it, my ass was in bad shape.

"I'm sorry, Mr. Fendi. This little bandit opened the childproof gate and got out. I told her momma she was going to get out." Our nanny and housekeeper came in and picked Chanel up from the floor.

"It's okay. Just sit her up here so she can stop crying. It's hurting my feelings."

"Are you sure? I don't want her to get a hold of any tubes or anything. Ms. Dream will have a fit. You got me in trouble rolling them blunts for you." I wanted to laugh, but it hurt. She placed my daughter on the side of me in the bed. The tears and crying immediately stopped.

"See, this all she wanted was to get up here with her daddy. Where is Dream? I called her, and she still hasn't come to see what I wanted.

"Ms. Dream left with Miyani. Do you need me to do anything for you?"

"I'm cool. Just bring her sippy cup."

I really wanted to tell her to call Dream and tell her to bring her ass home. Instead, I just chilled with my daughter. I thought about what Miyani said and knew she probably needed some air. Dream was overwhelmed, and I had made the situation worse. At the same time, I felt some type of way behind her leaving and not saying shit. It's too much going on in the streets right now for all that shit. I'm going to let her make it this time because I know I've been hard to deal with.

"YOU NEED TO STOP HOLLERING, Fendi. I understand that you're upset. Cussing and being mean will not help this situation." My mother was trying her best to make a nigga feel better, but I was pissed. Dream's ass had been gone for two days. She left out of the door with Miyani and never came back.

"Call Dream!"

"I called her already, and she said she's having me-time.

A woman is entitled to have some days to herself. Me, grandma, and Versace are here holding shit down. Let Dream have a minute to herself. She's overwhelmed, Fendi." I hit the bed over and over again, which only hurt me more.

"Yeah, she can have some me-time, but not while her nigga laid up like this! Dream needs to bring her ass home and take care of her nigga! How the fuck is she going to take a fucking personal day and leave?"

"Fendi, you need to stop hollering at me like I'm not your mother! Now, Dream told me everything that I needed to do. Just calm down, and I'll fluff the pillows the way you like, I'll cook the broccoli and cheddar soup, and I'll rub your feet. Just stop with your bullshit. This is not helping the situation, son. Allow me to help you. I want to help you!" My OG was damn near pleading with me, but I wasn't trying to hear it.

"Thanks, but no thanks. You won't do it the right way. Dream is the only one who could do those things right. Make her come home, ma."

"Boy, you done lost your god damn mind! I can't make her come home. Dream made it perfectly clear that she'll be coming home when she gets ready. Your ass is the reason why she needed a break. You're mean as fuck, Fendi!"

"Are you going to go get her or not?" I didn't have time to hear none of the shit she was talking about. Dream needed to bring her ass home.

"No, I'm not!"

"Then you can get out too! Where my brothers? I'm sick of all the women in this fucking family! You're my own mother and won't go get my baby! I'm lying up here in pain, and I need her. You want to see me in pain like this. Ma, please go get Dream and make her come home. I promise

I'll be nicer. I'm just frustrated as fuck! Dream is the only one that can make me feel better."

"Nigga, are you about to cry?" Prada said as he pushed the door open, laughing. He and G were standing there like this was the funniest shit they heard.

"This ain't the time for this bullshit! Go get Dream right now! Put her ass in the trunk if you have to. I don't give a fuck how y'all get her. Just bring her ass here."

"Thank God! Y'all are here. Let me go call Dream. I'm sick of his shit!" My mother walked and slammed the door. Good, her ass better call her. I'm so damn mad I might push through the pain and go get her ass myself.

"Nigga, you need to chill the fuck out! Here smoke this shit and calm the fuck down. We got some shit to show you." G handed me a blunt and a file at the same time.

"Is that those niggas that hit you up?" Prada asked.

"Hell yeah! That's them pigs. How did y'all find that out?"

"The shit was actually easy. We spoke with Big Joe and found who the motherfuckers were. They're from the Narcotics Unit. Apparently, there's an order to kill us on sight. Imagine that! Motherfuckers want us dead!" G spoke as he clenched his fist.

"Yeah! This shit crazy, but we're built for this shit. War motherfucking ready!" Prada added.

"I have to hurry up and heal! These niggas tried to take me out of my glow. My daughter was in the car with me, and I can't let that go. That's the part that fucks me up the most."

"Don't trip, lil Bro. You know we got you without a doubt. In the meantime, I want you to heal up, take your meds, and do everything the physical therapist said. Let the family handle the rest. Plus, you're the best man at my wedding. I need both of my brothers to stand beside me."

"I got you, big dog. Don't leave me out of the loop with anything pertaining to these fuck niggas. With that being said, are y'all going to get Dream for me? You niggas know I would do the same for y'all. Don't hurt my baby. Just shake her up a little."

"Nigga, your ass crazy! If we make Dream come home, then we'll be in the doghouse. I'm not trying to be beefing with Miyani."

"Shit, I'm already in the doghouse. Gavin is not fucking with a nigga period! I can't tell you the last time she licked this motherfucker like a lollipop!" I damn near bust my stitches laughing at this nigga Prada.

"Man, bring your silly ass on! We got you on that Dream situation." I knew G was going to handle that business for me. I'm glad they at least got eyes on the niggas that hit me up. Now, I can heal and get back to the fucking money.

NINE

GIVENCHY

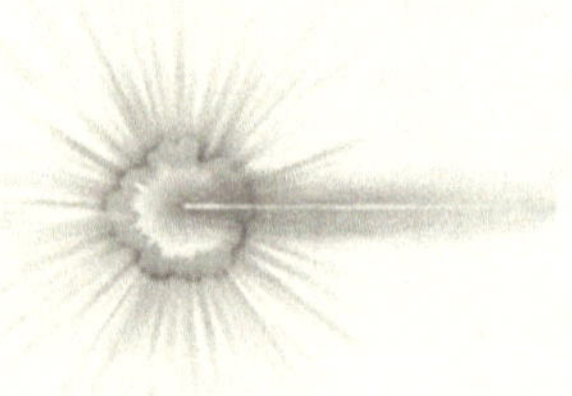

A nigga had been running nonstop since all of this has transpired. Putting them bitch ass police on ice was my main priority. Since I had that under control, it was time for me to deal with the India situation. The bitch thought she was in hiding, but she was really in plain sight.

When India and I were together, we had so many joint business ventures, not to mention properties all over. I was still in possession of all those properties. I just made it a habit to rent them out to families. One house that I never rented out but kept vacant was a house in the Hamptons.

India always talked about living out there. The way we rocked back then fucks me up right now. It's still hard to believe that this bitch was the fucking law. The shit fucks me up every time I look at my daughter. India is a deceitful ass bitch. I told her don't ever think she's smarter than me. I'm always ten steps ahead of my enemies. Right now, this bitch was public enemy number one. I had to keep my knowledge of her whereabouts under wraps from my family.

My mother had her own hidden agenda behind getting at Melissa and India. Honestly, we all do. It's just that me getting at her is crucial for the sake of Gianna. She's not to be trusted. How could you ever want a relationship with your daughter with vendettas against her father? The bitch got to go, and it has to be at my hands. I think I'm entitled to be the one that puts a bullet in her fucking skull.

India had gone into federal custody to help bring Melissa down. The bitch was the biggest rat I've ever seen in my life. It won't be long before I smoke Melissa out of the hole she's hiding in. It's time to end these miserable ass hoes existence.

"THIS IS NOT COOL, G. She's not ready to go back home." Miyani was pissed at Prada and me because we were trying to talk Dream into going home.

"Calm down, beautiful. Actually, it is time for Dream to go home. She's proven her point. Fendi gets it, and he's sorry."

"Put your shoes on, sis."

"Prada, you better leave me the hell alone. You and G need to go over there and take care of Fendi. I'm sick of his mean ass talking to me like he's crazy. He wants to be crazy, so I'm showing him crazy."

"Right now, is not the time to be on your Petty Betty shit. I'm sorry, sis, but you got to go home. Prada is going to take you home. Miyani, tell Dream you'll talk to her later."

I hated to do it this way, but Dream needed to go home. Fendi needed her, and with her nigga is where she needed to be. I don't judge how people move in their relationships. At the same time, if some shit ever happens to me, Miyani better hold shit down. Not saying Dream's not holding it down. It's just that she almost lost him. By God's grace, he's still here. You have to love people while they're here.

"Are you serious, Givenchy?"

"Yes, Miyani! I'm serious. Now walk Dream out, or Prada is going to trunk her. My brother wants his wife home?"

"So, if I decided I need some time away from you, Prada and Fendi would trunk me?"

"My brothers would get you back to me by any means necessary. Let's not get to thinking crazy, beautiful."

"Maybe I haven't been thinking at all." Miyani rolled her eyes and walked away.

"What the fuck that supposed to mean?" I tried to go after her, but Dream grabbed me.

"No, bro! Y'all are not about to be into behind my shit. It's cool, friend. Don't be mad about it. G and Prada just want me to go home and tend to their brother. It's cool. I'm taking my ass home. I miss my house anyway. Come on, Prada. I'm ready. Your ass better not make my friend cry either!" Dream pointed her finger at me before hiding out the door with Prada. I'm glad her ass willingly went because Prada was eager to trunk her ass.

My mother had requested that all of her grandkids

spend the night with her, which I was happy about. That woman is busy as fuck. I never thought anyone was as busy as my granny was, but Chanel got Gladys beat. I've had eyes on her since she's been back home. I know all about her having Dream and Miyani out here on that crazy shit with her. I was all for my mother and my girl getting close. One thing I know is that Miyani loves me. She doesn't have to prove her loyalty to me. I know she's a loyal woman.

Since we had the house to ourselves, I decided to kick back and blow a blunt. It was rare that I could smoke in the living room like this. Miyani has a fit when I don't blow weed out in the garage. As I smoked the blunt, I couldn't help but think about the statement Miyani made. A nigga needed to know if that's how she really felt.

Entering our bedroom, I heard the shower running. I couldn't help but gaze at Miyani's sexy body as she showered. Letting the toilet seat down, I sat on it and continued to watch her. We locked eyes, but neither one of us said a word. She turned her back to me and tried to ignore the fact that I was in the bathroom. Once I smoked the rest of the blunt, I took off my clothes. She wanted to act mad, so I needed to give her something to be mad about.

Opening the shower door, I stepped inside and cornered her. The hot water was raining down on both of us.

"You mad at a nigga or something?" I said as I placed kisses on the back of her neck.

"No. I'm not mad at you, Givenchy." Her back was still turned to me, so I roughly turned her around.

"Look me in my eyes when you lie to me." We were making eye contact with one another. I took that as an opportunity to grab her face and kiss her passionately.

"I'm not lying."

"There you go lying again." Pushing her up against the wall, I spread her legs. A nigga's dick was ready and rocked up. Taking one of her legs, I wrapped it around my waist so that I could have easier access to that pussy.

"Mmmmmm!" She was moaning out in pleasure, and I only had the head in.

"You mad at me?" I pushed my dick in farther as I bit down on her neck.

"Noooo! I'm not mad at you." She buried her face in my neck as I slammed all the way into her. Lifting her off the floor, I pressed her back up against the wall. I begin to slow stroke her with the dick, making sure to hit that spot every time.

"Fuckkkk!" I manage to say in a low tone. Miyani pussy was gripping my shit with each thrust. It's like since she'd given birth to our son, the shit even better.

"I love you, Givenchy. Don't stop! I'm getting ready to cum," Miyani spoke seductively in my ear as I began to bounce her up and down on the dick.

Fucking Miyani made a nigga feel so damn good. Her ass was so flexible that she was always able to take dick. I could be beating her shit out the frame, and she would tell me to fuck her harder. That shy female I fucked for the first time was long gone. Miyani could take a dick with no problem, not to mention do this motherfucker with precision.

"Do you love me, or do you love this dick?"

"I love both of y'all! Oh, shit! Nigga, I'm coming right nowww!" she moaned loudly, and I could feel he juices run all down the dick. I didn't have time to do no pulling. I came right along with her.

After releasing all my seeds inside of her, a nigga wasn't done just yet. I could still go another round in the pussy, so we took the shit to the bed. For hours, I fucked the mad right up out of her ass. She was mad as hell at me behind the shit with Dream. Instead of addressing the shit, she wanted to hold it in and be stubborn. That shit won't fly in a relationship with me. If you're mad, let's address that shit. I don't believe in going to bed angry with your spouse. She might as well put that shit out there. At the end of the night, we're going to fuck and cuddle until we fall asleep.

AFTER A COUPLE of hours of fucking nonstop, we sat up in bed, smoking and watched the new season of *Narcos*. Since we were chilling, I thought it was only fitting I let her know about the business trip I had to go on.

"Check it out. Babe, I need to go out of town for a couple of days. Some business really needs to get handled. It can't wait." Miyani's demeanor changed instantly.

"When will you be leaving?"

"First thing in the morning."

"Are you serious right now? Why would you wait to tell me this the day before?"

"I didn't tell you because I didn't know until this morning." Miyani tried to get out of the bed, but I pulled her back so that she wouldn't leave, and I guided her on top of me.

"We're supposed to go cake tasting tomorrow. This is our second time canceling. I really want your input on things."

"You don't need my input on things, beautiful. I trust your decisions. How about you take Versace with you? It would be good for her to spend time with you. She needs to be around a strong woman outside of Chanel. I'm sure you can give her some etiquette lessons." I could tell Miyani wasn't feeling it, but I knew she would do it for me.

"I got you, babe. How long will you be gone?" She leaned forward laid her head on my chest.

"Only a couple of days, I'll be back before you know it. While I'm gone, I want you to stay indoors. Don't go anywhere without Butta, Gunna, or Nettie. I've already given them a heads up about keeping an eye on you. Please listen to me, Miyani. Don't go out alone, beautiful. There are many people out in these streets trying to get at us. If they can't catch us, they'll catch the people close to us. Look at me and listen to what I'm telling you. I'm rich, powerful, and I got one of the baddest bitches out here. These niggas would kill for this good life that we live. I need you to be aware that a motherfucker will murk you to get to me. They will murder our kids if given the opportunity. You see, we're no longer living in a time where women and children were off-limits. Niggas are out here hungry, and they don't give a fuck who they got to kill to get that bread.

This is why it's imperative to have someone with you at all times. Promise me you won't go out unless you have to. If you have to go out, take someone with you. Are we clear?"

"Yes, G. I hear you." I placed a kiss on her forehead and loved all over her until we fell asleep. I needed all the rest I could get for this damn trip I had to take.

THE NEXT MORNING, I woke up early and caught a private flight out to South Hampton. I was ready to get this shit over and done with. It fucked me up as a man to leave my future wife and kids to go deal with a bitch from my past. The only way I could move forward with my new chapter was to close the old one.

"Good looking out on getting me this information. I appreciate this shit, Sal."

"Don't mention it. You helped me with that problem I had out in Chicago, so it's only fair I return the favor."

"Good looking. I'll have that sit-down with you before I head back home."

I shook hands with my business associate Sal Bucci. He ran a faction of the mob out in Jersey. Over the years, we've made each other a lot of money. It was through him that I met this cat by the name of Thug that was doing big shit across the fucking United States. Only the richest of niggas in the game could solidify a spot at the Bosses Roundtable. Just knowing The Alexander family had received an invitation let me know we were verified in these streets.

Sal had put some of his people on India until I could make it out here. His connections with the State's Attorney office helped me to see exactly what was going on.

After parting ways with Sal, I headed over to the property where India was hiding. Right now she was out of the house in a meeting with the government. This was my chance to slip inside and wait for her ass to come back. So that she wouldn't know I was inside, I had my driver drop me off outside of the community gates. Walking up to the house, I knew I needed to buy my baby Miyani a house. Here it was I had purchased this rat ass bitch a home in the Hamptons. The bitch didn't deserve anything I did for her ass. My baby Miyani deserves the world, and I intend to give her just that.

IT HAD BEEN HOURS, and nighttime had fallen. A nigga had been in the house for damn near ten hours before India arrived. I had smoked blunt after blunt to ease my mind. My phone had been going off like crazy, but I ignored it. Right now, I needed to focus on the task at hand.

"Now, I know I sprayed in here before I left!" India cut the light on and was like a deer in headlights.

"What's good, rat? Have a seat." I grabbed my gun from the table and placed it in my lap. Tears poured from her eyes, but it meant nothing to me. The bitch could save the tears because she was heartless.

"I'm sorry for everything, G. I just wanted to get to know who my birth mother was. I had no idea Melissa was holding your mom or sister hostage. As a matter of fact, the moment I found out, I went to my old superiors about it. That's the only reason how I ended up right back working with the police. I was telling the truth when I said I was done with that part of my life. All I wanted to do was come back and be with my family, but you wouldn't give me a chance, not with her in the picture.

"Your sister's name is Miyani. Don't be afraid to speak her name. You weren't afraid when you were plotting with your miserable excuse for a mother. Tell me something. Why does Melissa treat Miyani so fucked up? To my understanding, Butch is both of y'all daddy. She birthed both of y'all, so why does she hate Miyani? Give me some shit I can work with. Maybe I'll consider sparing your worthless ass life."

I know this bitch knows something about Melissa's plans and whereabouts.

"I don't know anything, Givenchy!" India started to cry harder, but I didn't give a fuck. She needed to know that I wasn't here to play with her deceitful ass.

"I don't know why Melissa hates Miyani. As a matter of fact, I don't know why she hates either of her daughters. It's not just Miyani or Gavin. She hates them both. The only reason she fucked with Gavin was because of who her father was."

"Speaking of Malcolm, did she kill that man?"

"Yes, she was poisoning him with arsenic for months until he collapsed. She didn't expect shit to go down the way it did. Not only did she call Gavin over there for her son's grandparents, but she called her to sign insurance papers as well. Melissa has been trying to get her alone to make her do it. She hasn't been able to do it because Prada doesn't let Gavin out of his sight. Both Gavin and Miyani have inherited money from Malcolm. From what I was told, she found documents that showed when he died, and everything would go to his daughters and nothing to her. That's when she started to poison him slowly. She didn't expect him to die before talking to Gavin about making her the trustee over their money."

I shook my head at the very thought of the bitch Melissa. Like what's this evil bitch issue with her daughters? I'm happy as fuck that I got my baby away from her ass. It didn't take a rocket scientist to know that she had killed Malcolm.

"Your ass is not too bright, are you? I understand you wanted to get to know your mother. At the same time, did it ever occur to you that she didn't give a fuck about you either? She only fucked with you because she needed you. Your rat ass knew it too, but you didn't care. At the expense of your daughter's wellbeing, you would hurt her father. Bitch, you fucked over me, not the other way around. It is what it is, though. Let's play let's make a deal. You tell me where Melissa's at, and I'll let you live." I stood up and moved closer to where she was sitting.

"I don't know where she is."

"Stop fucking lying! Them people had you on her ass. I know for a fact you know where the fuck she is at. Now tell me before I put a bullet in your head! I pressed my gun to the middle of her forehead.

"Promise you won't kill me, Givenchy!"

"Now, you know I'm a man of my word. Tell me where Melissa is."

"She's over in the Heights at her mother's house. If she's not there, she's more than likely running up behind Butch. That man doesn't want Melissa's ass, and from the looks of it, he never did. He's in love with Chanel."

The moment she spoke my mother's name, I pulled the trigger. India's brains flew all over the curtain behind her. It was as if a weight was lifted off my shoulders killing her ass. The bitch had been a pain in my ass from the moment she popped back up. With India gone, my daughter can live a fulfilled life with Miyani as her mother. I've already started the process for her to legally adopt her. Gianna is going to be so happy when I tell her all about it.

Usually, I would call in a cleanup crew, but I needed to get rid of the bitch myself. There was no coming back from the hole I had put in her fucking head. This situation required me to get my hands dirty. The bitch played with my heart, so I had to snatch her rotten soul.

GAVIN

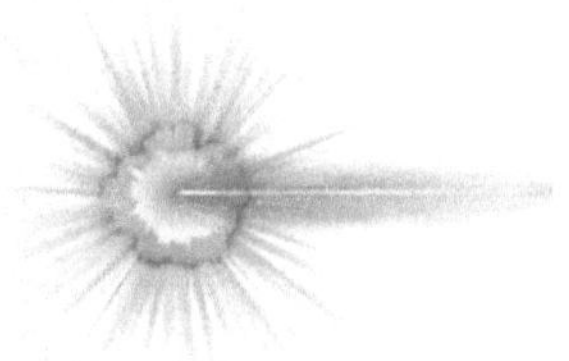

I walked around my house, trying to find every pill bottle that I could. One thing for sure and two for certain, I wasn't dealing with another man who does drugs. Prada handles himself very well in front of his team and the family. However, at home, I can see how much this shit is affecting him. That's when he does bring his ass home. I love Prada, but this nigga is around here a full-blown pill head. His family speaks on the way he pops Percs like its normal. Nothing is normal about this shit. I watched Carlo disintegrate before my very eyes. I was too afraid to speak up to him as a woman. He was my husband, and there was a time when shit was good. Despite his whack ass parents and their true intentions for me, allowing him to do as he pleased to keep the peace ended up fucking me in the end.

With Prada, I want a future. In order for us to have a future and have a happily ever after, shit has to change. Prada's fucking brain is fried right now, so it's up to me to handle this shit.

"Damn, sis, that's a lot of fucking pill bottles," Miyani said as she looked inside of the garbage can in the kitchen. I had dumped all the pills I could find down the toilet and the garbage disposal.

"I'm glad you're here to witness this. Prada swears that I'm exaggerating about this shit."

I sipped from my wine glass and tried to calm down. G was out of town, and her spoiled ass just had to get out of the house. That man hadn't been gone a good twenty fours, and she was losing her mind.

"Girl, this shit crazy. I'm so proud of you. Just stepping up and voicing your opinion without fear is so dope."

"Bitch, who said I wasn't scared. That motherfucker is crazy, but I love him so much."

"I know what you mean. Givenchy is everything, and I can't wait to walk down that aisle and officially become Mrs. Givenchy Alexander. At the same time, I feel like being with a man of his caliber overshadows me as a woman. Let me rephrase that. It overshadows me as Miyani. I feel like I've lost myself in loving him. At the same time loving him completes me. It completes me like dancing does. It's as if I can't function without that man. I don't know if that's a good thing or a bad thing. What if I get so lost in Team Supreme and forget what's important to me?"

"I'm sorry to tell you, but we're already lost in Team

Supreme. Look at me right now. I love Prada so much that I'm risking my sanity to save him. Our lives have changed for the better, Miyani. Prada makes me feel everything Carlo never allowed me to feel. As bipolar as this relationship is, I'll take it any day over getting my ass beat. Noonie hurt, embarrassed, and humiliated you in front of the world. After everything you did for that man, he shitted on you. I watched you not be able to sleep or eat behind that shit. Miyani, you're a different type of woman. You could have outed him to the world, but you didn't. Instead, you took the high road. You worked on yourself and bossed up on his ass. Now he can't stay out of my DM asking about you. I didn't want to tell you because of the drama that it would cause."

"What? That nigga had better get the fuck on before G kills his ass. One would think that after he pulled his gun on his fraud ass, he would get the hint. Noonie doesn't want the problems that come behind fucking with me."

We both fell out laughing because that nigga had a death wish doing that shit. I've told him repeatedly to leave Miyani alone because she's getting ready to get married. He insists on trying to get in contact with her. A hard head makes a soft ass, or shall I say bullet in your head. That's exactly what G is going to do if he even thinks a nigga is sniffing up behind his "beautiful".

The sound of Prada's loud ass music let me know he was home. My heart started to race because, in a minute, he was going to realize I had thrown out his pills. The nigga was about to get ignorant, and I was ready. My son was with Prada's mother, so he wouldn't be here to see us humbug. We were definitely about to come to blows.

"Let me lace my shoes up!"

"For what?"

"In case this nigga gets to cutting up because I'm going

to cut up with him." I leaned over and started tying up my VaporMax.

"I'm laughing my ass off. Bitch, this nigga done made you violent." Miyani laughed at my ass, but I was dead ass serious about this shit. I was not about to take this shit lightly.

"I'm not about to let his behavior get out of control like I did with Carlo. We're about to nip that shit in the bud right now."

"I'm going to leave so that you can handle your shit. Lexx is about to pick me up and take me back home. G is going to start blowing up my phone in a minute. I love you and call me if that nigga gets stupid."

"You leaving already, sis? I just got here."

"Yeah, bro, I need to make it home before your brother starts calling. I'll see y'all at Sunday dinner." Miyani hugged both of us and left out of the door.

Prada didn't say a word to me. His ass went right up the stairs to the medicine cabinet. I drank the rest of my wine straight down.

"Yo, Gavin!"

"Yes, babe?" I answered as I walked up the stairs to our bedroom.

"Don't babe me! Where the fuck is my shit at?" Prada was holding an empty pill bottle with the meanest look on his face.

"I threw them out."

"What the fuck you say you did?" He swiftly walked in my face, and I pushed his ass back, creating some space between us.

"Don't walk up in my face like that. I threw them away because I'm tired of your ass being high all the time. When was the last time we spent time with each other? Prada, you've been so high out of your mind that you've been staying away. You haven't been coming home. You've been at your mother's house every night this weekend. You only come here to grab the pills and money out the safe. I've been trying not to say anything with all the shit going on. However, we need to discuss this shit."

"The only motherfucking conversation I want to have with your ass I about my shit. Who the fuck told you to do some shit like that? Do I walk around this motherfucker throwing your shit? How would you like it if I start throwing your shit away?" He went inside of our bathroom and started knocking all my makeup on the floor.

"Stop it, Prada!"

"Hell, nah! You don't like how it feels when somebody touches your shit, do you?"

"It's not the same, nigga, and you know it. I threw shit out because it's ruining you. Can't you see the shit is ruining our relationship?"

"That shit don't hold no weight over our relationship. Stop being so damn dramatic."

I observed him walking around searching the room. The shit was so sad to see that tears welled up in my eyes. He flipped the mattress and grabbed a small bag with pills in it. Seeing him throw the pills in his mouth angered the fuck out me. He was really showing me he didn't give a fuck. I needed to show his ass I didn't either.

"I guess you've made your choice. I love you, but I give up. I love the fuck out of you nigga, but you can't stay here."

"Fuck you mean I can't stay here? This my fucking house."

"No, nigga! This is my fucking house. You made me move out of the house I got from you. It was you who wanted me to be here. I'm not going anywhere. Take your dope fiend ass right back over to your momma's house. I'm done, Prada."

I tried to rush out of the room, but he stopped me. The nigga pulled me back like the matrix and threw my ass on the bed.

"What's this shit you talking about being done?"

"Stop it, Prada! I'm serious." He was roughly tugging at my pants, trying to get them off. He had me pinned down with one hand while he pulled them down with the other.

"You trying to leave a nigga for no reason!"

"Get your ass off of me!" I was fake squirming, trying to get out of him off me.

In a way, I welcomed it because this was the closest we had been lately. It had been a minute since we had sex, so a bitch was yearning for the dick. At the same time, I'm mad at his ass. Prada has to understand that I'm not tolerating this drug shit.

"So, you don't love a nigga anymore."

"You know I love you, but I can't deal with that drug shit. I don't want to be with you anymore if you can't give that shit up. I've been through enough, and I don't want to go through anything else. For the sake of my sanity, I have to choose me no matter how much I love. You promised me that you would always be here for CJ and me. Lately, you've been an absent fiancé and father. You introduced me to a vibe I fell in love with, so now it's your job to maintain it. It's either us or them pills."

"I choose you and my son. I'll always choose you and him."

Prada got off me and kneeled to remove my shoes and pants. He removed his clothes and roughly pulled me to the edge of the bed. He gently spread my legs apart and began feasting on my pussy. I bit down on my bottom lip while staring at the top of his head. This nigga was giving me that head Jody gave Yvette in the movie *Baby Boy*.

"Ohhh, shitttt! Right there!"

I grabbed the back of Prada's head and grind all in his mouth. He was assaulting my clit with his tongue. My body became so warm as I squirted all over the place. The feeling was so good that I couldn't alert him if I wanted to. My eyes rolled in the back of my head as I rode the waves of ecstasy.

"Bend your ass over!" On command, I got up on all fours and gave him that death arch — the one that was about to have him coming faster than he expected.

"Ahhhhhhhhh!"

"Shut the fuck up!" Prada had rammed his fat ass dick so hard it felt like some shit shifted. He had roughly grabbed my waist and started roughly pounded in and out of me. The shit felt good but hurt at the same time.

"Wait, Prada!" I tried to push his ass back a little because he was really trying to kill my shit. Those damn pills had him fucking me like an animal.

"Ain't no motherfucking wait! You said you were leaving a nigga. So, I'm about to give you this dick for the road!"

"Ahhhh! I'm not leaving! Stop Prada. Ohhh, Fuckkkk!"

"Yeah, that's right! Let me punish that pussy!" Prada grabbed my hair and wrapped around his hands as he went crazy all in the pussy. All I could do was let him have his way until we were both coming at the same time.

I'm not going to even lie. This was one of the best sex sessions we've ever had. I fell flat, and he laid on my back, continuing to stroke me slowly. He was giving me the strokes that make your damn eyes well up with tears. Them strokes that make you sprung off dick game alone. Prada had a point to prove, and he was definitely proving it to me. I hoped and prayed he was telling the truth about stopping. He thinks he slick. He done put that dope dick on me and made me give him another chance. I suggest he takes this shit seriously because I'm not playing about the drug use. When he came in here tonight, I was fully prepared to fight. I'm happy that we decided to fuck instead. The shit made me feel good as fuck, but I was still in my feelings.

For the rest of the day, we chilled in bed and talked about things. After our conversation, I felt like he was telling the truth about not taking drugs anymore, which made me sleep much better. Prada had no idea how worried I've been about him. It's as if he's a totally different person since his mother has returned. He's been on a pill and alcohol binge ever since. I wonder if she knew she was stressing my man the fuck out. The more I stared at him while he slept, the more I knew I needed to talk to Chanel. My man's soul is disturbed, and she has no idea. She had yet to reach out to me for a sit-down, so I decided to just pop up at her house. We both love the same man, so we're going to have to come to common ground when it comes to how he is handled.

NERVOUS WASN'T a word as I stood ringing the bell on Chanel's doorstep. I promised myself I would never come to her house uninvited again. This shit is for the love of Prada. If I didn't love him, I wouldn't even be here. I have my own problems with my evil ass mother. This lady ain't shit like they described outside of her looks. Her ass is more like a menace to society instead of a saint. Dream and Miyani told me about her ass. I see why her sons and momma don't give a fuck.

"Well, don't stand there, come in?" She stepped to the side and allowed me to come in.

"Thanks, Chanel. Can we talk real quick?"

"Hello, Gavin. I didn't know we had an appointment."

"We don't. I just needed to talk to you about Prada."

She gestured for me to follow her, and I did. Her house was raw as fuck. Prada has got to hire me an interior decorator for the house that he doesn't know he's buying me yet. I deserve I gift behind his foolishness these days.

We walked inside of her office, and I was even more in love. This shit screamed boss, and I wanted parts.

"What about my baby? Is he okay?"

"No. He's not okay. Prada is addicted to popping Percocet. This is not something he does here and there. He pops them all day and every day. His behavior at home has gotten out of control. Now, I'm not here as a daughter-in-law pleading for help. I'm here as his future wife. I need to have a conversation with the woman who l have to share his heart with."

Chanel looked surprised at what I said. Before responding, she poured both of us a glass of champagne. I stared at her as she flamed her cigarette up like she was a nigga.

"Lay it all out there on the table. It seems like you came here on a mission. Let's get that shit accomplished."

She took a sip of her champagne and stared at me intensely. I made sure to hold my stare, as well. Ms. Glady's taught me well, and she taught Chanel, so I knew I was holding my own.

"I respect the fact that you're his mother, but I need us to be on one accord when it comes to his care. Yes, I know that he is a grown ass man. At the same time, he's still that eight-year-old boy that saw his mother gunned down. Since then, he has blamed himself for running away and not getting help. As fearless and crazy as he is, he felt like a coward. Knowing that you're alive has fucked him up. Ms. Chanel, he's eating them damn Percs like they're candy. I just found every pill bottle I could find in the house and threw them out. It would really help if you did the same. I don't mean any disrespect, so please don't take it that way. On some real shit, my courage comes from the love I have for that man."

"Thank you for being supportive of him. I know that he's fucked up, and it hurts me. That's why I just leave him alone when he falls to sleep over here. It helps me to bond with him. Building relationships with my sons are so important to me. When I first found out that my sons were dealing with Melissa's daughters, I planned to kill both of you. My mind changed seeing how much they love y'all. You, Miyani, and Dream are something special to those boys. How can I not love y'all? I promise you have my support with this situation. I'll do my part and make sure he stays off that shit."

"Thank you so much, Ms. Chanel."

"No problem. It takes a lot of guts to step to me. Had you been a bitch I didn't like; I would have killed you and held my son while he mourned you. Now hurry up, we have somewhere to be." She stood to her feet and knocked back the glass of champagne.

"Wait a minute. Where are we going?" This lady thought she was slick, getting ready to try to take me out to do some crazy shit. I knew I should never have brought my ass over here, trying to be a down ass bitch.

"Just come on. I'll tell you where we're going when we get there."

I just shook my head following this crazy ass lady. There was no telling what the hell she was about to get me into. At the same time, I was anxious to see where we were going. I knew that Prada would be calling, so I decided to put my phone on silent. I'll just tell him I didn't know because it was down in my purse. I left out of the house without an escort, so he would definitely be calling. We've basically been laying low with all this shit going on in the streets.

AFTER ABOUT AN HOUR OF DRIVING, we ended up in Hoffman Estates. I got somewhat antsy because this is where Carlo and I lived before I left.

"What are we doing out here?"

"I'm glad you asked. Prada talked to me about the nigga Carlo and the bitch Esha. I'm happy my son handled that nigga's parents. However, we must kill Carlo and Esha. We can't leave anyone breathing that tries to hurt this family. Death to your enemy is the only thing that will allow you to sleep a night. A motherfucker with a vendetta that's still breathing is a big risk."

"Maybe we should call Prada." I felt kind of uneasy being around Carlo without him. I haven't been around him alone since the day I left.

"This is not Prada's beef. That hoe shot you, and that nigga put his hands on you for sport. You need to go in there and handle your business. Come on, have some fun with your mother-in-law. Think of it as our first bonding session."

This was one crazy ass lady. She had this grin on her face like the Joker. As much as I wanted to get the fuck out of dodge, I knew I couldn't. These motherfuckers had to go.

"How do we know they're in there?"

"Because they're tied up in the basement."

She opened up a secret compartment and handed me a Glock.

"Ms. Chanel, you're too much for me." We both laughed and got out of the car.

It was a good thing I was dressed for the occasion. I looked good as fuck. I couldn't wait for Carlo to see me. This melanin dripping is something serious around this motherfucker. I'm still mad as hell at Prada, but my baby definitely upgraded me. I'm not speaking monetary wise. That man elevated the fuck out of my confidence. Carlo had me thinking that I was ugly and no one would love me but him. Look at me now. I'm in love with the best thing that ever happened. It doesn't even matter that he's a damn pill-popping animal. Prada still treats me one hundred percent better than Carlo ever did.

When we walked up to the house, Chanel went inside with the keys. I wanted to ask so many questions, but I know she's just going to be evasive with the answers. Fuck it! Let me kill these bitches and get it over with. Maybe this is what I needed to fully move on with my life. As long as he was still breathing, CJ and I would never be one hundred percent safe from the bullshit.

Once we were inside, I looked around the room and knew Esha had decorated. It looked like a damn zoo with all the zebra stripes and leopard prints. Carlo must have been getting in tune with his black side now. If I had did some shit like this to our house, he would have busted my damn head.

"I just have one question, Gavin. How in the hell did you end up with that damn white boy?"

"I was a political pawn in my mother's wicked game of power. She didn't even care about him beating my ass."

"Don't worry. Her ass will be dead soon enough. Let's

get this shit over with. Prada is going to kill me for having you doing this. He is hell-bent on keeping your hands clean of blood. You're a part of Team Supreme, so it's a must you have blood on your hands!"

I continued to follow Chanel through the house and down to the basement. I had to hold my breath for a minute because the smell of blood permeated the air.

"What the fuck?"

My eyes were wide as saucers looking at Prada with a blunt dangling from his mouth and a big ass electric chainsaw in hand. Looking down at the pile of limbs, I became sick as fuck. Carlo's head was turned my way and his eyes were wide open. The shit had me about throw up everywhere.

"How did you get in here, Prada?"

"I've been on they ass for about a month. I told you I wanted to kill these motherfuckers myself. Why the hell you got her with you on bullshit?"

"Boy, you better pipe the fuck down. I understand you're grown, but you're not grown enough to be cursing at me. Shit, I wanted her to get some get back against these motherfuckers! That damn Butta. I know he's the one that told you about this shit. I should have never told his ass to snatch them up for me."

"Hell yeah, he told me. Your ass is busy just like grandma."

These two were going back and forth as if it wasn't a pile of limbs in front of us. They were speaking as if it was nothing. All I could think about is what the fuck have I gotten myself into. This family is sick as fuck.

"Baby, remember I told you I was going to torture these motherfuckers for hurting you?"

"Yes."

"I'm a nigga that keeps my word. I love you more than anything in this world. The last thing I'm about to do is lose the only woman that understands and loves me for me. I'm done with that pill shit. You gotta believe me, love."

"I believe you, Prada." I couldn't help but walk over to him and place a passionate kiss on his lips.

"Y'all can do this shit later. Let's get the hell out of here. I wanted Gavin to blow some shit up today. Prada, you fucked up my plans."

"Oh my god! Let's get out of here, Ms. Chanel."

I didn't want to do anything but get the hell out of here. Esha and Carlo's body parts were freaking me the fuck out. I'll never get this sight or the smell out of my memory. There is no way I'll be able to eat after seeing this shit.

"Y'all get out of here. I have to clean this shit up. Go home, baby. I'll be there in a couple of hours."

Prada and I exchanged a kiss then I headed up the stairs. I could hear Chanel and Prada talking but didn't care to listen. I wanted to be as far away from that basement as I could be. Looking around the living room, my eyes became fixated on a huge picture that sat in the middle of the wall. The same picture used to be at the house we shared. It wasn't a picture at all. Actually, it was the safe where he kept his money and important papers. He could never remember numbers, so I'm sure the code was our son birthday. Gently, pulling on the sides of the frame, it instantly opened. I quickly placed the code into the safe and it opened.

The safe was filled to the brim with money and folders. Removing the files, I placed them in my purse. Looking around, I went in search of the kitchen for a garbage bag. It took me a couple of seconds, but I found what I needed.

Rushing back into the living room, I quickly dumped all the money in the garbage bag.

I didn't leave a dime behind. All of this shit was going to my son. This was his fucking money. Carlo wasn't shit to him when he was alive, but he made him a rich ass kid in death.

Later that night, I laid in bed waiting for Prada to come home. A weight had lifted off my shoulders. Carlo and his parents were dead. Finally, I could breathe freely without worry about the Carlo situation. Now all I need is to fully close the chapter with my mother. She's the cause of all this shit and is hiding out like a coward. She needed to show her face and deal with the consequences of her actions.

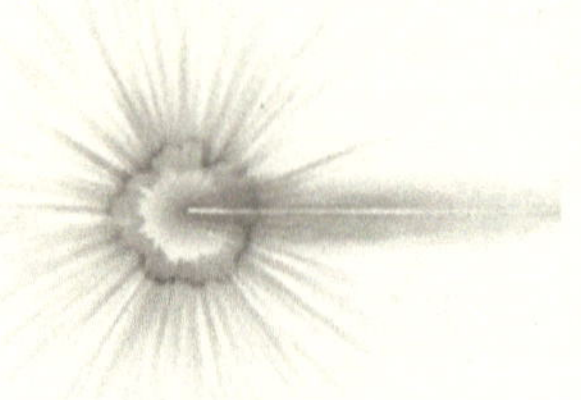

"Good morning, Ms. Mills?"

"Good morning, Portia. I grabbed coffee and donuts for you to sit out. We have about thirty showings today. Givenchy wants all the spaces filled by month's end, so you know we're team no sleep for the next couple of weeks, right?"

"I already know, boss lady. I'm ready, though. Thanks again for giving me this job."

"Stop thanking me. I'm always willing to help a mother

in need. Remember, you can drop your daughter off for ballet lessons on the house."

"Ms. Mills, you are too much." I laughed at Portia and headed to my office.

Supreme Suites was finally open and ready to move tenants in. Givenchy put me in charge of leasing the apartments. I hired Portia on as my assistant after she came into the Chanel House for shelter. Once I interviewed her, I learned she was homeless with her five-year-old daughter. It broke my heart. She was the reason why Givenchy wanted the Chanel house opened. It was for women and children in need. My baby went all out trying to honor his mother's legacy. Now that she's alive, he wants people to know how dope she is. All he does is brag on her. I've never seen him so happy. He's like a big kid in her presence.

I'm so happy that I was able to execute Givenchy's vision for Supreme Suites and the Chanel House. The entire city was talking about the Alexander family is giving back to the community. As much as they are hated, they are loved. I couldn't be prouder to be a part of something so damn illegal and dope at the same time.

Checking my e-mails, I came across one from Noonie. I quickly deleted it without even looking at it. I had no idea why he was trying to get in contact with me. In a minute, I'm going to have to tell Givenchy. The only reason I haven't said anything is because I don't want him going out and murder Noonie's stupid ass. This man just didn't give up. He was never persistent like this when we were together. What the hell is he fucking with me for I have no clue. One thing for sure and two for certain, that nigga can't breathe the same air as me. He's wasting his time trying to contact me because I'm never going to respond.

I didn't get a chance to sit down good before Portia was

telling me someone was here for me. My first appointment wasn't until ten in the morning, so I had no idea who it could be. When I walked outside to the lobby, I was surprised to see Mr. Shaw. He was my father Malcolm's attorney for as long as I could remember. He was rocking two black eyes. All I could think about was who had whooped his ass and why in the hell he was here.

"Hello, Mr. Shaw. What brings you here?"

"Ms. Miyani, can we go somewhere private and talk?" He was obviously nervous and afraid.

"Of course. Come into my office. Portia, get G on the line and tell him to come here."

I quickly walked him to my office. This shit felt off to me.

"Thank you so much. I've been trying to get in contact with you and Gavin since your father's death. Your father left each of you some crucial information. I've been holding on to it for dear life. Everything was okay until your mother and some men showed up to my office, demanding that I give it to her. You see, Malcolm didn't leave Melissa anything, and she's upset. He left everything to you girls. Please take this folder and sign off on all the checks and get your sister's signature as well. I have to get this out of my possession before she gets ahold of it.

"You good, baby?" Givenchy rushed inside of my office with his gun out.

"I'm fine, G. Put that up."

"Damn, man, who beat your ass?" I held in my laugh, looking at him observe Mr. Shaw's face. I'm not going to even lie. He was fucked up.

"This is Malcolm's attorney. He says that Malcolm left everything he owned to Gavin and me. He didn't leave Melissa anything, and of course, she's pissed. She had some guys do this to him trying to make him turn over the things he left us."

"Miyani, you have to take these things. I told Melissa they were in a safe deposit box at the bank, but only you or Gavin can open it. I told her that I would do what I could to get into it."

"So, you're here to get access to it for that bitch!"

"No, sir! Mr. Alexander, I'm here to give them what's rightfully owed to them. That lady is ruthless. She methodically killed Malcolm over the course of six months with arsenic. Melissa doesn't deserve to get anything. I only told her that to buy me time to find Miyani and Gavin. The only reason I knew how to find Miyani was seeing you guys on the news about this place. I'm trying to protect my daughters. She threatened to kidnap them from school and sell them to men out of the country."

"If you help me get Melissa, I'll pay you one million dollars."

"I can't take your money, Mr. Alexander. I'll help you get her. All I ask is for protection for my family. Malcolm was a good friend of mine before he got with that she-devil. I told him from the beginning not to mess with her, but he didn't listen. He felt sorry for her because she was pregnant with Miyani. The way she treats this girl is ridiculous. She's the reason why Malcolm welcomed her into his home. It was all to give Miyani a good life. I want her dead. This world is too good for a cruel ass woman like that."

Just hearing Mr. Shaw speak on how Malcolm loved me really made me feel good. Melissa tried to act as if it was such a bad thing that he wasn't my father. I'm just glad I know that he loved me. Not even in death can she take that from me.

"Thank you so much, Mr. Shaw." I got up from my

chair and walked around to where he was so that I could hug him. He didn't have to do this. The man risked his life for Gavin and me, and now, he was willing to help G get at her.

"No problem. Sign those checks in the folder and make sure you deposit them immediately. I can't risk that money going to anyone it doesn't belong to."

"Don't worry about that, Shaw. I'll make sure she and Gavin get them deposited. Let's talk about getting Melissa to come back to your office. Handle that baby and take Gunna with you."

"I can't go right now. We have potential tenants."

"Have Portia do them. She needs to learn all of this shit because we don't do the logistics. All we do is worry about the residuals. Give me a kiss and go handle that." G kissed me and gestured for Mr. Shaw to follow him.

I wanted revenge on Melissa, but I knew G would never allow me to do anything. It was everything to him to protect me. That man loves me so much he's willing to lose his life and freedom behind me. I've never felt love like this before. When a man loves a woman this way, a bitch can't do shit but let him lead. I'll allow him to lead me because he's worth it. Many niggas out here want you to follow them, but they don't know how to lead. My baby is a true boss ass leader. He holds court out in these motherfucking streets, not to mention dropping big dick off in me in between the sheets. I have the type of man bitches would kill for. Givenchy loves me, and I know it because he shows it every day. It makes my pussy wet watching him plotting to kill people or make moves. I'm so fucked up about his gangster ass ways. I couldn't wait for him to come home tonight. My baby needs some of the best sloppy toppy a bitch could give to him.

Opening the folder, there were two checks for five million apiece for Gavin and me. There was a letter with my name on it from Malcolm. I quickly opened, and all I could do was cry while reading it.

My beautiful Miyani,

If you're reading this letter, that means I'm no longer alive. First, I want you to know that I've loved you from the moment you came into this world. You were my daughter, and that's why I gave you my last name. No one could tell me anything. When I met your mother, Melissa, she came off as a single mother in need. I intended to help her get on her feet and make sure she was set for when you were born. I was being a friend, but I ended up falling in love with her cruel ass. If I had known what I learned later, I would have let her ass stay being single.

When we got together, I had no idea she was into sex trafficking. Contrary to what people think, I had no idea in the beginning. For the sake of my political career, I kept quiet about it. For years, I tried to keep the shit under wraps. Little did I know, she and other political figures in Chicago had been operating an international sex ring.

While searching for tax documents, I came across pictures of women and children that were up for sale. I also found a black book, which should be enclosed in this folder. It holds the names of all the political figures that are a part of the sex ring. Keep it and use it when you need to. These motherfuckers will pay whatever you ask for in an effort to keep their political status. When I was alive, I couldn't expose anyone because it would hurt my family and me. Melissa and her evil ass ways ruined everything. The last thing I wanted to do was hurt you girls any more than I already had. I know that money changes nothing, but please accept it as a peace offering. From the bottom of my heart,

I'm sorry that I never protected you girls. I'm so happy you and Gavin are with those Alexander boys. I know that they'll give you girls and my grandbabies the lives we never gave you girls. Both of you deserve better than we ever gave you.

I'm so sorry, my beautiful Miyani. I hope that you can forgive me for everything. Please don't live this life feeling any type of way about your mother. Let God handle her. Live the life that you deserve. I don't know if I'm in Heaven or Hell. Wherever I am, just know that you're my daughter, and I love you forever and after that.

Love, Your Father!
Malcolm Mills

I SAT in my office crying my eyes out. This shit had my heart hurting, but it also gave me closure. Just to know I meant something to that man is everything. I understand it was all Melissa being the mastermind in ruining our relationship, but I still feel like as a man, he could have done better. After reading this letter, I fully understand. Melissa was holding that man hostage with her bullshit. I hope and pray G finds her ass and ends her miserable ass. I pray my father lives in the clouds amongst the angels. He gave my heartless mother sanctuary for her unborn child, and her selfish ass ruined it.

WALKING around my new dance studio felt so good. It was finally finished, and the first classes would be starting soon. All of my girls were going to be so happy. My new spot was big enough for recitals now. I've already planned our first one out. I've already concluded that I'm no longer dancing. The injury I sustained was too much trauma on my foot. I've decided to hang up my dancing shoes and allow my amazing staff to do the teaching. As much as it hurts me to do that, I know that I need to. I can't keep injuring my foot anymore. Its bittersweet stepping away from that part of me. I'm just grateful Givenchy has given me so many streams of income that I won't miss it as much. Dancing was my refuge from this cold world, and now that I have Givenchy to be my refuge, I'm content with that.

"So, this is what I have to do to come see you?"

I turned around and locked eyes with none other than Noonie.

"Would you please me leave me alone? I'm in a relationship and getting married in a couple of months. Why are you trying to get in contact with me so badly? For the sake of your life, it would do you good justice to leave me alone.

"I'm sorry for what I did to you. I just want to tell you I'm sorry."

"Apology accepted." I tried walking around him and to my car, but he blocked me.

"Damn, Miyani! Since when you don't have time to talk to me?"

"Since you left me and got married to your pregnant mistress. Move, Noonie. I don't want anything to do with you. Please leave me alone. I'm getting married and happy. I love my fiancé. He's more man than you'll ever be. I was there for your ass, and you left me for that hoe. I'm good. I forgive you. Just move on with your life and stop contacting me. My fiancé doesn't play about other niggas contacting me."

I pushed past his ass and quickly walked to my car. That nigga had lost his mind fucking with me. Niggas are a trip. That man has a whole wife and two kids. Why he's fuckin' with me, I don't know. I just hope he takes heed and leaves me alone. I couldn't wait to get home and tell Givenchy. With Noonie popping up at my new studio, I knew it was serious. He shouldn't have come to my place of business. That shit is not cool. Actually, he shouldn't be trying to get in contact with me at all. If his low down dirty ass thinks he's about to fuck up my shit, he's got another thing coming. I'm good on all levels.

"CAN WE TALK FOR A MINUTE?" I asked Givenchy as I walked into his man cave. He was chilling smoking a blunt while watching *Scarface*. It was damn near three in the morning, and I couldn't sleep.

"Of course. Come over here and sit with me."

When I walked over to him, he handed the blunt to me. I sat down, and he quickly put my feet in his lap. He placed a kiss on each foot as always. I continued to smoke on the blunt as I stared at my feet.

"Do you like them?"

"Of course. You know my favorite color is royal blue. Next time I want you to get them sunflower yellow." The way this man chooses the colors on my toes is sweet and hilarious at the same time. Givenchy is truly one in a million with this shit here.

"While I was leaving the studio today, Noonie was outside. He e-mailed me, but I didn't respond, and he's also been e-mailing Gavin."

"Hold up! How long this nigga been trying to get at you?"

"Well, today was the first time he came to the studio. He's e-mailed me about three times since last month. I'm not sure how long it has been with him e-mailing Gavin. I just feel like today was too much, and I needed to let you know."

"So, if he wouldn't have shown up today, you wouldn't have said shit? The nigga's been e-mailing you and your sister. You were supposed to tell me the first time that fuck nigga tried to get in contact with you. What? Were you trying to spare his life?" G stared at me intensely as he took a long pull from the blunt.

"No. I wasn't trying to spare his life."

"Don't lie to me. Right now, you're lying to me, and I can see it. Watch out!" He knocked my feet off his lap and walked out of the man cave. Had I known he was going to be mad at me, I never would have said shit about it.

I sat there for a minute before going in search of him. When I made it upstairs, G was in the bathroom. I attempted to walk inside, but he slammed the door in my damn face. Instead of trying to talk to him, I climbed my ass in the bed. I didn't do anything wrong by not saying something sooner. Hell, I wanted to keep the fucking peace. It's not going on with this family, but at the time, I didn't think it was serious to worry him at. I should never have told him shit. Gavin was gone be mad as hell at me when she finds out I told Givenchy Noonie was e-mailing her ass too. Fuck it. If I'm in trouble, her ass is too. I couldn't be in the doghouse by myself.

As soon as I powered my Kindle on so I could finish my book, G walked out. He was pissed at me for real. The vein in his neck was protruding so bad I thought it would burst. He climbed in bed and turned his back to me.

"Don't ever keep some shit like that from me again. You hear me, Miyani."

"Yes, Givenchy, I hear you."

"Don't read that shit while you in the bed with me either. You don't need to be reading about no other niggas while you laid up with me." I busted out laughing because he was so serious about that shit.

"Now, you know you're the only nigga I think about."

I wrapped my arms around him and placed a kiss on the back of his neck. He pulled me closer to see him, and I snuggled under him. I melted into his mean ass. Although he had simmered down a bit, I know that G was still mad at me, that added with the fact that he was going to fuck Noonie up.

I took a deep breath before I got out of my car. It was taking everything in me to show up at Silk's house unannounced. He hadn't been around since we exchanged words about two weeks ago. Silk had been irritating the fuck out me. I appreciated him helping Prada to rescue me, but his presence was becoming too much. It's not because I didn't want him around. It was more so looking into his sad ass eyes and knowing I caused him so much pain.

Back then, I didn't want to be tied to just one man. Silk was determined to turn me into some bitch that watched soap operas all day, raised kids, and catered to his ass. His black ass had me fucked up. Gladys Alexander didn't raise me like that. I loved me some Silk, but that man wanted to dim my shine. He didn't feel good being the nigga who bitch was the Queen of the Chi. That's why we fought so much, and that's how I ended up fucking on Butch's crazy ass.

Butch let me be who I wanted to be. In the beginning, shit was cool until that hoe Melissa popped up on the scene. Everything went downhill from there, and it was all my fault. I fucked up my life, my kids' lives, and Silk's life. The crazy part about this was that I didn't love Butch's ass. Silk had my heart. He just wanted me to be a stay home wife and mother. I wasn't ready for it all of that. Not treating Silk right is one of the biggest mistakes of my life.

As I headed up to his door, "Sexual Healing" by Marvin Gaye played in the background. I laughed on the inside thinking about how much he used to love him some music. Silk opened the door in a tank top and pajama pants. I turned my nose up at the cigar dangling from his mouth. I hated the smell of that shit, and he knows it.

"What are you doing here, Chanel?"

"Can I come in and talk to you for a minute?"

"I'm sorry. Now is not a good time. I have some company."

"Let's be clear, Silk. Nothing has changed about who I am around this motherfucker! I'm the same Chanel that didn't play with your hoes then, and I'm not about to play with them now. You need to send that hoe on her way. I got some shit I need to discuss with you."

"Chanel don't come around here with that bullshit. What in the hell do you have to talk to me about? You made it perfectly clear you didn't want me around."

"Yeah, I said that, but I was mad. I don't give a fuck

what I say to your black ass. Make it your business to check on your sons and grandkids. You just reunited with them. After all of these years, one would think you would want to be around all the time."

"I'm going to get out of here. I'll call you later, Silk."

I looked the young bitch that walked out of the house up and down. He needed his ass whooped fucking with a girl his damn sons' age.

"Yeah, you get on out of here, and you could lose his number. He's a married man with children and grandchildren." I pushed his ass back inside and walked in behind him. I slammed the door so hard the whole damn living room shook.

"Really, Chanel? What the hell you want with me?"

"I came to give you this. It's all yours." I handed him the envelope, and he opened it.

"I don't want your money, Chanel. A nigga is set for the rest of my life." Silk handed the check back to me and sat in the recliner.

Silk was being so stubborn right now. I should have known he wouldn't take it. This man's pride and his ego is still the same.

"Look, I know that what I did to you back in the day wasn't cool. Outside of the fighting and cheating, you were a great father and provider. All you wanted is for me to be the dutiful wife. All I've ever wanted to do is run shit. I did what I could to survive after being shot and exiled by the United States Government. Haiti gave me what I couldn't achieve out here. Please! Take these five million dollars as a peace offering."

Silk stared at me as he took a sip from his glass.

"Again, I don't want your money. Do me a favor, though? Tell your sons and your mother who you are today.

They deserve to know that you are the Queen of Coke over in Haiti."

Hearing him say that made me sit down on the couch across from him. I knew I should never have come over here and continued to keep my distance. Silk always thinks he knows everything.

"It's not that easy, and you know it."

"Make that shit easy like it was easy to fuck Butch! You ruined our family all over some dick. While I was out making us more business connections, you were laid up with him. Everything this family is going through now stems from the past. Your fucked up past is the reason why I did time, and our kids went into foster care. Yeah, Gladys raised them, but I would have loved to raise my sons. You come back into their lives, and they love you. I come back into their life, and I'm scrutinized behind laying hands on you. My sons think that I used to whoop your ass for sport. They don't know how fucking disrespectful of a woman you were to a nigga!"

"You know what? I don't have time for this. I did what I had to do out in Haiti to survive. Take this money Silk and leave this shit alone."

"Here's a word of advice. Givenchy knows something is up, and he's getting closer to it. You need to tell him the truth. I'll make sure to be hands-on with sons and the grand-kids. Just do me that favor and be real. The Chanel Alexander I fell in love with was crazy about her sons. They've mourned you for twenty years. For the sake of your relationship with them, I advise you tell them the truth."

"You're talking like I'm lying to them. Everything that I told them was the truth."

"You just left out the most important part."

I shook my head at Silk ass out of frustration. He was

really trying to act as if I was keeping some big sordid ass secret from my family. It was just something I didn't speak on to them.

"You're over exaggerating."

"Okay. I'm over exaggerating. Tell me this, though. Are you going back to Haiti?"

"I have to go back to Haiti."

"I can't believe I loved your selfish ass. After all of these years, you're still a selfish bitch."

"You know what. Let me get out of here before it be a gunfight. I'm not going to be too many more bitches. I refuse to explain to you why I'm moving the way that I am. I'm going to leave this check right here. Please take it, Silk." I hurried up and got out of his fucking house. That fine ass nigga still has the power to make me feel like shit.

WALKING into my mother's house, I observed her sitting in her favorite spot — in the damn window being nosey. For a minute, I just stood looking at her beauty. She hasn't aged too much. If her hair weren't all gray, one would never know she was up in age. Ms. Gladys was still young in her mind. I still can't believe she gets every Jordan shoe that comes out. My boys keep her so fly. I admired the way they all love each other. Since I've come back, I've observed their dynamic. She's not just their grandmother. She's their mother. They go to her for everything, especially Prada. I know that she loves them all equally, but he's her pick.

I'm not jealous or anything. In my absence, she raised my kids, and I'm appreciative of that. I'm glad that she taught them this street shit where I left off. They have built an empire, and I wasn't here to have a hand in it. The more

I've been here, the more I've realized that they don't need me.

"Why are you looking at me like that?"

"I'm just looking at how beautiful you are." I sat on the couch next to my momma and started looking out of the window. It reminded me of all the old times we used to sit in this very window.

"What brings you over here?"

"Nothing. I just wanted to come over and see what you were doing. Versace said she's been calling you, but she couldn't get an answer."

"That's because I wasn't answering for her ass. She thinks I'm a babysitter, and I'm not. I get my grandbabies on my time, not when their parents want me to. Versace's got a lot to learn about me." My momma flamed up a Black & Mild, making me cringe. Why must she smoke them stanky ass things?

"I told her you weren't getting that baby. Ever since she started working down at the club with Dream, she has forgotten she's a mother."

I wasn't really feeling her working down there anyway. Versace has never been around that type of element. In Haiti, she was sheltered.

"Well, I hired her a nanny. I have shit to do I can't be sitting around watching kids. I'm glad she's down at the club with Dream. It's time for her to earn her way and learn the family business. With y'all being back home, it's time I teach her some things so that she can bring in some earnings. Everybody in this family contributes to this family. Since y'all are back home, we can elevate in business even more. The whole family is together, and it's a beautiful thing."

My mother's eyes danced as she spoke. She was thrilled

for us to be back. It hurt me to know that I was about to break her heart.

"Versace and I aren't staying here. I have a business in Haiti, and I have to get back to it. After I kill Melissa and Butch, we're going back."

"What you mean going you're going back?"

Hearing Givenchy's voice, I knew this shit was about to go left. I realized Givenchy, Prada, and Fendi had all came in and listened to what I was saying. The looks on their faces spoke volumes.

"I have to go back to Haiti. Had they not kidnapped us and brought us here, I would still be over there."

"I don't understand this shit, Chanel! You get shot and survive. You're sent over to Haiti with some damn man. You marry him, and he gets killed. Then the people that made it so you would be in Haiti brought you back to the states. This is your home. Make me understand why the fuck you have to go back? For twenty years, we thought that you were dead. It rocked our world to find out you were truly alive. I'm starting to think your ass really wasn't being held captive over there."

"In the beginning, I was being held captive. Once I married Christopher, he didn't treat me as a captive. He treated me as his wife. When I became his wife and helped his failing coke business, I became Queen of Coke.

That's who I am in Haiti. They worship and fear me over there. I run coke through Haiti, and I supply the entire state of Florida. So, you see, I have to go back. I'm free, and I can come to Chicago whenever I feel like it."

The room was filled with complete silence. I wanted one of them to say something. My mother got up and walked out. Prada and Fendi went behind her. Givenchy stood in the middle of the floor, staring at me intensely.

"Do whatever you have to do." His face held no emotion as he spoke. Without so much as another word, I watched all my boys leave. The last thing I wanted was for them to be mad at me, but of course, they were pissed.

"I'm about to go to the boat. I'll talk with you later."

They were all being so dramatic about this. I sat in deep thought for as long as I could before leaving. All I could do was pray that my family understood. The money was the motive, and I had to do whatever I needed to in an effort to keep it flowing.

THIRTEEN

DREAM

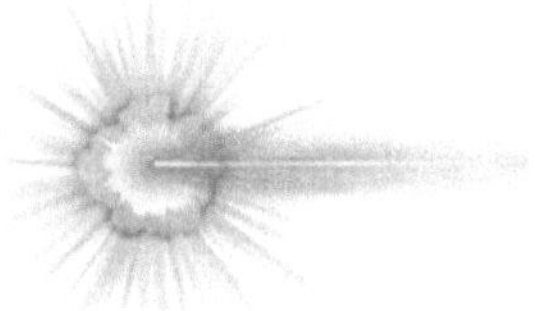

Pissed was an understatement for the way I was feeling. Fendi had missed my prenatal appointment for the second time. At first, I understood he couldn't make it because he had to catch up on work. This time for him to miss it had me pissed. This shit feels like when I was going through my first pregnancy alone. Of course, that time, it was my fault. This time around, though, my nigga is just too damn busy. If that weren't enough, he still hadn't healed all the way. The moment he got enough strength to walk around, his ass was out the door. I swear this was why I didn't want to have another baby right now. Fendi just had to knock me up, and my dumb ass let him.

I probably wouldn't be so mad if his ass would answer the phone for me. I'm convinced this nigga loves humbugging with my crazy ass. On the ride home from my appointment, I had to pass Team Supreme Headquarters. I had to piss so badly, and there was no way I was going to make it home without pissing on myself.

It was a good thing I knew the security code to get inside. There was a car out front, but it wasn't familiar.

The moment I got inside; I ran trying to get to the bathroom. Without knocking, I busted inside of the door.

"Oh shit!" Gunna yelled as he hurriedly pulled his pants up. This nigga was fucking the shit out of Nettie's girlfriend, Lexx, on the sink.

"I told you this was a bad idea." She scrambled, trying to pull her damn clothes on.

"What the hell y'all doing? Nettie is going to go the fuck off. Oh my god! Why did I have to be the one to see this shit?

"Please, sis! Don't say shit. I promise I'm going to talk to Nettie. Just don't say anything."

"Let me in here before I piss on myself." I damn near pissed on myself. As I sat on the toilet, all I could think of was the drama that was sure to happen behind this. I couldn't wait to get home to call Miyani and Gavin. This shit here is beyond me.

When I was finished, I headed out of the bathroom. I observed Gunna consoling Lexx. This is more than just some quick ass fling. These two motherfuckers had been fucking. Lord, it was definitely going to be some shit behind this.

"I could have been anybody coming in here. Why are y'all fucking behind Nettie's back?"

"Man, sis, it ain't even like that. About three years ago, I went out to Miami to handle some shit for G, and I met Alexis while there. We fucked with each other the whole weekend, and the next thing I know, she's calling me talking about she's pregnant. My life was too hectic to raise a baby, but I made sure to send her money monthly. We never really knew shit about each other, and I wanted it to stay that way. When she popped up with Nettie, I couldn't bring myself to say shit."

"So, the little boy that you brought over to the house with you and Nettie is Gunna's son."

"Yeah." Lexx was clearly upset about it.

"Stop crying. I was once in your shoes to a certain extent, not the whole gay relationship thing. I went through something with Fendi as well. I'm not judging either of you. Lord knows I've done my share of dirt. However, y'all have to come clean about this. Team Supreme is going through a lot right now in these streets. We don't need rifts in the family. I'm not going to say anything to anyone, but y'all can't keep moving like this. The shit is not cool."

I was dead ass serious about what I was saying. Nettie thinks she's a whole man around this motherfucker, not to mention a gangster. She's going to want to fight Gunna and whoop Lexx's ass.

"I need to meet up with the crew. Can you please drop Lexx off at home for me?"

"Yeah, bro. You and I are gone talk about this shit later." He kissed me on the cheek and rushed out of the warehouse. Gunna and I had become close during the time Fendi was healing.

"Don't be looking all sad now! Those fuck faces you

were making screamed happy. Come on so I can drop you off. Gone and do that walk of shame."

"Oh, Lord, Dream. I busted out laughing as her ass walked out of the warehouse.

"I'm just fucking with you. Girl, if I added all the damn walks of shame I've had to do, it would be equivalent to walking a marathon."

As we drove away, the car was silent. Lexx was just staring out of the window. I really didn't know what to say to her. However, I did want to know why she hadn't told Nettie. Last time I checked, they were in a full-blown relationship. I fucks with Nettie, and I feel like if Lexx doesn't want her, she needs to let her know.

"I'm not trying to be in your business or tell you what to do. However, you need to tell Nettie about this. It's going to hurt her, Lexx."

"Fuck, Nettie! Nothing is going to hurt her heartless ass. Nettie nose ain't squeaky clean either. She's been fucking with that hoe Niara under everybody nose."

"Wait a minute! Are you sure? I thought that was her sister or her cousin."

"Niara is no damn kin to Lexx. Her grandmother took Niara in when they were teenagers. Niara and Lexx have been messing around for some time."

"You know she used to fuck with, G."

"Yeah, I know. That's part of the reason why I say Nettie's not shit. I went through her phone, and they are in a full-blown relationship. They've been dealing for years. Silly of me to think that Nettie was serious about this relationship with me. Come to find out she's only been fucking me to make sure I keep the drug operation going on at the jail. That's what I get for trying to be a lesbian. I swore off men when I got pregnant with my son. Gunna hurt my heart telling me he wasn't ready for kids. Yes, my son has never wanted for anything. At the same time, he deserved his father in his life. Since the moment Gunna realized I was living here, he has stepped up in a major way. Nettie ain't shit, Dream."

I continued to drive in complete shock, and my ears were burning, listening to the shit she was saying. This shit was going to end all bad.

"Nettie is so loyal to Team Supreme. She's been with them forever. This is so unbelievable."

"Well, believe it. I don't trust, Niara. It has nothing to do with her fucking Nettie. I can't judge her for her sneaky pussy when I have it as well. My issue with her is how she's always badmouthing Team Supreme. She does the shit in front of Nettie, and she doesn't say shit. I didn't think anything of it at first. It wasn't until I found out they were fucking that the shit became clear. Nettie is gone off that hoe Niara."

The more Lexx talked the more I wanted her ass to keep talking. I knew she was telling the truth. This wasn't a woman scorned. She wasn't just saying shit and making excuses to make her infidelity okay. Lexx was real with her shit. I needed to know more about what was being said by this hoe. If she has a beef with Team Supreme, then the hoe definitely has a beef with me. We're one band one sound around this motherfucker.

"I know she hates Miyani because Givenchy chose her. When Fendi was in the hospital, we had to ban her ass from the room and being his nurse. I really don't know her like that, but she rubbed me the wrong way then."

"That girl is sick that she had to go back and work at the hospital. One day I was in the room, and they thought I was sleep. Niara was speaking on how G stopped her money flow by stopping her from doing runs. I flat out heard her ass say fuck Team Supreme."

"What did Nettie say when she said that shit?"

"Shit really. She told her to calm down, and in due time she'll be back to doing trips. I'll never understand why she said that. Givenchy has banned that girl from breathing the same air he breathes."

"This is some heavy shit. I don't even know what to say. Does Gunna know about this?"

"No. I didn't tell him anything. I'm new to working for Team Supreme. This is serious, so I don't want to be speaking on shit and cause a domino effect of drama. I felt comfortable telling you. At the same time, I didn't think it was a situation that was really serious until I found out they were fucking. Nettie is walking around advocating to G on Niara's behalf, and all along that's her bitch, and she's pussy whipped."

"Well, we both know being pussy whipped never ends well." I shook my head at this crazy ass lesbian love affair. I'll stick to dick. Ain't no pussy about to have me stressed out.

"You know we need to tell Givenchy about this, right?"

"I know. I'm going to tell Nettie we're done tonight, and then I'll tell G. Please don't say anything just yet. I promise I'll tell her about Gunna and our son. Thanks for dropping me off."

"No problem, boo. You got my number, right?"

"Yeah, I do. Call me if you need me." I exchanged a hug with Lexx, and she got out of the car.

I had to sit for a minute before pulling off. My ass was floored hearing that Nettie and Niara were fucking. I wasn't even shocked about catching Lexx and Gunna in the act anymore. They were wrong too, but this shit with Nettie trumps it all. I prayed she wasn't plotting on the family. It was enough shit going on, and we didn't need anything else adding to it.

"WHY ARE you sitting here in the dark?" Fendi was sitting in the living room with the lights dimmed. He was drinking out of the bottle of Hennessy and smoking a blunt.

"I got some shit on my mind."

"Is there anything I can do? Did you take your medicine today?"

"Oh shit! I forgot. Go get it for me."

"You can't forget to finish those antibiotics. Your wounds haven't healed completely. This is why I didn't want you to go back to working so soon. Fendi, you know you can't drink alcohol while you're on antibiotics." This man was so damn hardheaded, and it made no sense at all.

"I know. I'm sorry, baby." I damn near broke my neck looking at him saying that. I had to feel his forehead to see if he had a damn fever. Clearly, he was sick apologizing so easily.

"Are you okay?"

"I'm fine, babe. You're right. As a matter of fact, you're always right. I'm just a wild ass nigga that's been able to whatever the fuck I wanted. I'm sorry for being so hard on you while I was laid up. No matter how many times I spazzed out on you, you didn't give up on my ass, except for when I had to make my brothers bring your ass home."

"Ms. Gladys and Chanel told me you were crying too." I laughed as I kissed him.

"Hell yeah! I had to do something to make them feel sorry for me. On some real shit, though. I do apologize whole heartedly. Outside of my family. I'm just happy that I have you and my daughter to come home to."

"Are you okay, Fendi? Did something go on today? Is that why you missed my prenatal appointment?"

"Oh shit! Damn, I'm so sorry, babe."

"I was mad at first, but I'm not mad anymore. The baby is growing properly, and we probably can see what the sex of the baby is during the next visit. We can discuss that later, though. I'm more worried about you right now. What happened today?" Fendi's whole demeanor was off. My baby was sad about something, and I could feel it. He wiped his hand over his face in frustration.

"Chanel told us that she's going back to Haiti."

"What! Why would she want to go back to a place that held her against her will?"

"That's because, once she married that Touissant nigga, her status elevated. She was no longer a captive. She became a willing participant, all in the name of having power. That nigga's dead, and it thrust her into his position. She's known as the Queen of Coke out in Haiti. I'm not fucked up about her going back for the sake of drug game. I'm fucked up in the head about her being gone all of those years without reaching out to us. I've been so happy about my mother being back home. Finding out I had a sister and a nephew put the icing on the cake. I couldn't help but spoil them crazy. G, Prada, and I have been out splurging, trying to make sure they have a comfortable life here. Not once did she ever say that she was going back. One would think that after being away from us for twenty years, she would never want to leave our side. You know what? I don't even give a fuck! Come lay with a nigga.

"I'm sorry, Fendi." Those were the only words I could muster up to say.

There really wasn't much I could do to console him. He has been going all out since Chanel came back home. The shit had me angry as fuck. Here she was walking around here testing our loyalty to her sons when she really should have been testing herself. Chanel is so wrong for this shit. These grown ass men need her more than ever. The fact that she can't see that angers me. It made me feel good knowing that my daughter would have a grandmother in her life outside of Ms. Gladys. She can't build a relationship with any of her grandchildren if she is back in Haiti.

For the rest of the night, I watched the father of my children toss and turn. My baby's soul was disturbed, and his mother was the cause of it. How could she do this to her boys? I felt like I needed to say something to her to try to get her to stay. Then again, I needed to mind my business. This was something that Fendi and his brothers needed to come to terms with. Maybe things would be better for everybody if she did go back to Haiti. Honestly, shit was smoother when her ass was dead. It was important for me to keep my distance at this point. To see my nigga so hurt has me wanting to fight, and I can't lay hands on Chanel. She's not the average hood mother. We would fuck around and be in a gunfight. Nobody got time for that shit.

FENDI

From the moment I had gotten well enough to walk around, I had been casing out the niggas who shot me. They were both creatures of habit. I had their daily routines down pact. Motherfuckers had no idea who they were fucking with. Niggas thought it was okay to shoot me. They should have killed my ass because I won't rest until I make them front-page news.

My phone had been going off repeatedly, but I wasn't answering for anyone. A nigga was trying to focus on the task at hand. I was following this nigga Pierce and Santos as they worked their beat. The more I followed them, the more I realized just what the fuck they were doing. The niggas were supposed to serve and protect. Instead, they were abusing their powers. These motherfuckers were basically robbing the local dope boys for their money and drugs. They would act as if they were arresting them when actually all they were doing was taking their money and drugs. These two motherfuckers had to go immediately.

The fact that they had orders to kill any Alexander on sight has me anxious. That's why I've been keeping a tight hold on Dream going out alone with my daughter. I would kill this whole city if something happened to my girls. Outside of my blood family, Dream is the only one I can depend on. I've been really fucked up to her. The more I think about it, the more fucked up I feel. Her mouth is out of control, but her heart is so pure. She's always had love inside of her to give. She just never met a real nigga to give it to until she crossed paths with me. I know Dream's not really happy about being pregnant right now. She's simply embracing it to make me happy. That speaks volumes to me. I also don't want her to do anything out of fear of me. The last thing any man should want is their woman being afraid to make decisions for herself. That shit not cool. Hell, I know damn well Dream was not scared of my ass. Her crazy ass will square up with my ass in a minute. What she doesn't know is that shit does nothing but turn me on.

"What's good, bro?" I dapped it up with my young bull, Dex.

"Shit! About to paint the sidewalk with pigs' blood. Get from around these parts. Hit me later. I got some shit in place for you and your crew. Good looking on this location. It's perfect."

"No doubt. Tell your grandma I want my grand back. She hustled the fuck out of me at the pool hall yesterday."

"I told y'all to stop gambling with my granny. She's a pro at that gambling shit."

These niggas will never learn. They love gambling with my granny. I've seen her break the hardest of niggas pockets. She's even come up on properties and cars when niggas couldn't pay up. I couldn't do shit but laugh at his dumb ass. She's been getting him out of his money since he was about thirteen. One would think he would learn by now.

I jogged up the stairs to the roof, where Dex had already set up for me. My brothers were going to be mad at me for moving without them. This was my vendetta, and I needed to handle it. My brothers know I'm about that action in these streets. Why they think I need them to do shit for me, I'll never understand. Givenchy and Prada can be pains in the ass — my grandma too with her real busy ass. She's the main one always out in the streets thinking she needs to settle our beefs.

Like clockwork, Pierce and Santos headed inside of Starbucks. That was my cue to get in position. I laid flat on the roof and looked through the scope. My hood was falling over my eyes, so I had to take it off. I needed to make sure I was able to get precise shots of those fuck niggas. I waited patiently down to the precise second they walked out of the Starbucks. As they both fully stepped out into view, I let off the first shot. It hit Pierce in the middle of the forehead. The second shot hit Santos straight through his left. They were dead before they realized what had happened.

Quickly! I gathered everything and headed out of the building. I could hear the sounds of people screaming and sirens in the distance. Before the police made it to block off the scene, I drove away. I let out the nervous air I had been holding in. I head straight over to the chop shop to get rid of the car and gun. The sound of helicopters and sirens could be heard across the city. After getting rid of the car and the guns, I headed straight to the crib. These pigs were about to have the entire city on lockdown, trying to find out who killed them fuck niggas. A nigga couldn't be caught out in the streets behind this shit.

"YOU DO KNOW you don't have to work, don't you?" I asked my little sister, Versace. She had been hell-bent on working and learning the business. Dream had been teaching her the ropes, and she had caught instantly.

"I know, but I want to open up my own clubs one day. The only way for me to do the shit and be successful is to start from the bottom. Plus, Chanel thinks I'm going back to Haiti, and I'm not. I love being here with y'all. It's so much fun, and I love it out here. Everything back home is always hectic. Being here makes me be able to experience what it feels like to be a part of a family."

"You know she's not going to like that, don't you?" Chanel was going to be pissed when she finds out Versace don't want to go back to Haiti.

"I know, but she has no other choice but to respect my wishes. I'm an adult with a child of my own. I can make my own decisions. I've been in contact with Gucci's father, and he knows that I'm not bringing my son back there. If he wants his family, he'll make the necessary sacrifices to be where we are. If not, it ain't no pressure behind these niggas — not even when he's your husband and the father of your child. Thanks for letting me learn the ropes." Versace kissed me on the cheek and walked off.

She had been hanging around Dream's ass for too long. That's exactly some shit Dream would say about a nigga. Versace's crazy if she thinks that man not gone come for his family. If he doesn't, he's fuck nigga to the fullest. Chanel is going to have a fit when she finds out Versace doesn't want to go back to Haiti.

I'm glad that she wants to stay. As a matter of fact, I think it's better Versace stays here anyway. There is no telling what Chanel has going on that we don't know about. The way she spoke about going back so casually didn't sit right with me. She was taken against her will and left over there, and the first chance she gets to being free to come home to her kids, she doesn't. Instead, she stays and becomes the Queen of Coke.

At first, I was in my feelings about the shit. I only vented to Dream about it. My brothers hadn't expressed their feelings verbally to me either. At this point in my life, I'm good whether she stays or goes. I've lived damn near all my life without a mother, so there is no need for me to act like I don't know how to now. It's just fucked up that she's been away for so long and ready to go away again. I'm just happy my daughter is still young and doesn't know what's going on. She doesn't need any disappointments in this life. I'm going to make sure she knows not to expect much from people in this world. It be your own people that give you grief.

Knocking back a shot, I observed Dream running shit. Every employee on the roster listened to Dream when she spoke. This was the first time I really watched how she ran shit. My baby was a natural ass boss. The more I watched her, the more I wanted to expand. We can open spots in Miami and Atlanta. Yeah, it was time for me to start being more hands on with this club shit. I've been sitting on a cash cow all of this time and hadn't taken advantage of it. Dream will be having the baby soon, and while she's down, I'm going to surprise the fuck out of her. My baby is about to get the best push gift ever times two. I have to make up for not being with her when my daughter came into this world. Dream deserves the world she never got from a family. It's only right I give her a dope ass love like she reads about in them messy ass books. I don't know why she's so into them damn book baes when she's got my pretty ass to wake up to every day.

My phone rang brought me out of my thoughts about Dream. I answered, and it was Prada telling me to make it over to the headquarters. He couldn't say what it was. That could only mean they were about to ask me about murking them damn pigs.

"Baby, I need to head over to this last-minute meeting with my brothers. I'm going to send Dex and his crew over here to help y'all close up. I'll see you at home later."

"Okay. Be careful, Fendi, and take it easy. Don't be out there. I'm going to try to wait up for you, but I'm so tired."

"You need to start preparing to let Versace and my grandma run the day-to-day operations. I don't feel good with you still working and pregnant like this. I understand that you like to be in control of things, but this is still a club. After this month, you're stepping back, so I advise you to mentally prepare yourself.

"Okay, Fendi." I was side eyeing the shit out of her, since when is she obedient?

"You're not sick or nothing, are you?" I reached out to feel her forehead, but she knocked my hand out of the way.

"Stop, fool. No, I'm not sick. I just agree I need to sit down and let them handle things. Don't take too long making it home. I love you."

"I love you too, baby." I kissed her on her forehead and got ready to head out. I'm glad I was high and tipsy. A nigga definitely needed to be intoxicated to deal with the shit Givenchy and Prada was about to say.

***

ABOUT AN HOUR LATER, I was walking inside of Team Supreme Headquarters. G and Prada were sitting at the table, passing a blunt back and forth.

"What's so damn important that it couldn't wait until tomorrow?"

"We have a big problem?" G said as he flamed up a blunt.

"What type of problem?"

"Did you know about Gunna and Lexx fucking around?" Prada asked.

"Hell nah! Gunna doesn't move like that. He knows that shit goes against the code. Does Nettie know?"

"I don't think so, but it really doesn't matter whether or not she knows. Loyalty to the team is what's at stake here. This shit is bigger than Gunna fucking Lexx."

"What's bigger than Gunna fucking Lexx?"

"It's two things that bigger. Lexx's son is Gunna seed, and Nettie's been fucking Niara for the longest."

Prada shook his head as he handed the blunt to me. I focused on G, and I could tell he's about to explode. I knew he didn't give a fuck about Niara. It was the fact that Nettie had crossed the line. Not only did she cross the line. She also crossed Givenchy, and you never want to cross that nigga. Yeah, shit is about to get real.

FIFTEEN

GIVENCHY

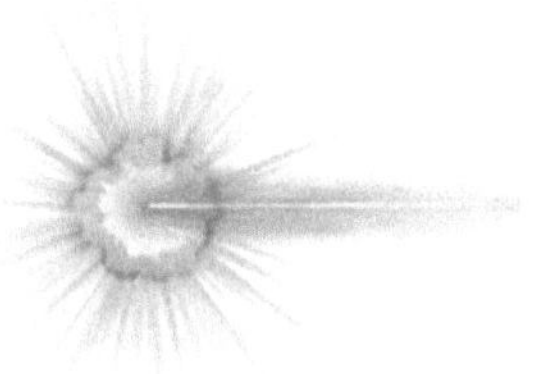

It had been a minute since a nigga was overwhelmed with this thing called life. The shit that was going on had me frustrated and out for blood. So many people were plotting against Team Supreme. I can handle beef in the streets. It ain't no pressure for a nigga like me when it comes to shit like that. I live for a good ole fashioned gunfight. It's one thing to be on high alert behind people in the streets, but it's something completely different when it's your family.

I'm happy my mother is alive and well. I'm even more pleased that she's home with us. Just knowing that she wants to go back to Haiti has me feeling some type of way. At the same time, who am I to be in my feelings about her wanting to leave. It's crazy that she wants to go, but I'm not about to wreck my brain behind the shit.

From the jump, I said there was so much more to the story than what she was saying. She conveniently left out the part about her being the Queen of Coke.

I've watched the way she moves, and she's greedy. She loves money, but she loves the power even more. The power she craves can be detrimental to everything I'm trying to do here. A lot of beef in the streets and heat from the FEDS that we've sustained is due to the shit she has done.

Now, don't get me wrong. I love my mother, and I'm happy she's alive. It's just that my brothers and I have built an empire in her absence. Her presence has brought a shift in the atmosphere. For so long, I've dreamed of how life would be with my mother. However, what I've dreamed of is nothing like the reality of it all. The grown man in me has to understand that she's not the mother I lost at ten years old. Even grown niggas need their mother.

The last thing on my mind was losing her, and we just got her back. If Haiti is where she feels like she needs to be, then so be it. As her son, I have an issue with her leaving, but as a businessman, I understand it's better for her to leave. I'll never express these feelings to my brothers. The hurt hits different with them, especially Prada. In due time, they'll be okay. They have lived damn near their whole life without her, so they'll be able to live the rest of it without her just like me.

Honestly, I have my own shit right here that I need to be worried about. I'm not about to worry myself with Chanel and all her secrets. Distance is necessary because right now, she's not looking very trustworthy. I don't give a fuck who a person is. If I can't trust you, I don't want you around me. I'm okay with loving her from a distance.

Team Supreme has always operated under the code of loyalty. When that loyalty is compromised, it's imperative to take the necessary steps needed to rectify things. This situation with Nettie has really fucked me up. I don't understand why she would be fucking around with Niara all of this time. It makes no sense at all. Back in the day, we all shared these bitches. Nettie is literally one of the guys. We don't treat her like a female. She knows how the fuck we roll. Ain't no beef behind no bitches with us. This is different, though. Nettie has played me like a sucker ass nigga.

I'm glad Lexx came clean and told Gunna about the shit. He came and expressed the situation with him and Lexx as well. I can't knock that man for wanting a relationship with the mother of his child. Nettie, on the other hand, is who I have a big ass issue with. I trusted her around my family, and I've made it perfectly clear that Niara is not to be around anything remotely close to me. Nettie defied me. Therefore, she now has to deal with the consequences that come with that. I would handle that shit later. Right now, I had other shit that was more important that needed to be handled.

<hr>

"I THINK we should just cancel the wedding and get hitched at the courthouse."

Miyani was so frustrated with the planning of the wedding. I told her to do whatever she wants. There was no budget, so I wanted my baby to wild the fuck out. A woman like Miyani deserves to have a wedding that people will talk about forever.

"I'm not the type of man that gets married at the courthouse. Hire a wedding planner if you're becoming overwhelmed. You should be having fun doing this, not worrying, and having second thoughts. I want to receive you the way a king is supposed to." I kissed her on the forehead and fixed my tie.

I'm headed to a crucial meeting at city hall. It was a must that I walked my ass in there looking like every dollar I was worth. I'm feeling like a gentleman and gangster at the same time. These people have no idea the chess move I'm about to play on their ass.

"It's just more work than I thought. I'm going to go ahead and get Gavin and Dream's help. I've just been trying to do everything on my own. Don't worry. I won't get so overwhelmed where I won't be able to enjoy planning it. I'm glad you want me to walk down the aisle. You never cease to amaze me. I never thought I would meet a man who just wants to give me all the things in this world. Who would have ever thought I would find you?" Miyani grabbed me by the face and kissed me passionately.

"I'm the one caught a blessing that day I met your beautiful ass."

"I hate when you do that, Givenchy. Please let me dote on you for a change. Every time I'm praising you for something, you turn around and praise me. Trust me. I'm flattered by that shit. Sometimes the king of the castle deserves to be praised, especially when he lets me sit on the throne."

Miyani grabbed a handful of my dick. I couldn't help but look at her ass with shocked eyes. At first, she acted so shy with a nigga. Not now! She takes the dick when she wants it.

"If I didn't have to go to this meeting, I would let you sit on this motherfucker now!"

"Speaking of this meeting, what is it a meeting for?"

"Let's just say, if all goes well, our lives are going to change drastically. My goal is to take this family to a higher level in life. Team Supreme is more than an organized crime family. We have the potential to change the world. With you beside me, I can run this city. Do you believe I have that type of power?" I stroked her cheek while staring into her eyes intensely. I was about to embark on a journey no gangsta nigga has ever been on, so it was imperative I saw into depths of Miyani's soul. A nigga really needed the praises she says that I deserve.

"Givenchy Alexander, you exude so much fucking power. I don't think you understand just how much power you have. Baby, when you walk in the room, you make niggas part like the Red Sea. They stop all conversations and wait for you to give the okay to speak again. Not only that, but you give back to the community. You have a heart of gold. You have the power to run the world, baby. It will be my pleasure to run it with you. Now tell me your plans."

"I'm going to be the next Mayor of Chicago!" I kissed her on the forehead and hurriedly left.

Miyani needed to be left with something to think about. Of course, I know the news has her fucked up in the head. She grew up in a fucked up political family. This may be the last thing she wants to be a part of, but rest assure she'll thank me later. I know y'all reading this shit shocked. Is this nigga really about to run for mayor? Hell yeah, I am. The city needs a real nigga like me. You see, there's a big difference between the type of politician I'm about to be and the ones we have now.

I'm going in this bitch as a known criminal with my rap sheet out there for the world to see. I don't have shit to hide. The streets know the real me and how I move. My campaigns will be filled with the truth, unlike the crooked ass politicians being elected now. You see, they run campaigns dripped with lies to get a vote, when all along they're running all types of schemes behind the scenes. They're taking taxpayers' money and dumping it into their personal accounts, all the while claiming to be for the people.

Yeah, I'm about to change the fucking game, and I have Malcolm Mills to thank for that. My family was going to go ape shit when I tell them what I have planned.

"GOVERNOR BRAGG WILL SEE you now, Mr. Alexander," his assistant spoke as she led the way to his office.

This nigga had me waiting for like an hour. I had the right mind to fuck him up when I got in there. As bad as I wanted to, I knew that I couldn't, at least not right now anyway.

About a minute later, we walked inside of a conference room. I smiled as I looked at the faces of who I requested to be in attendance. Their faces showed that they weren't too happy about being there. If I were them, I wouldn't be happy either.

"Let's get this over with, Mr. Alexander. What brings all of this on?" Governor Bragg spoke with a little too much bass in his voice. Instead of snapping his fucking neck, I pulled a blunt from inside my suit pocket. I flamed it up and blew it in his directions.

"This is a non-smoking building?" the treasurer Mike Monroe said while fanning the smoke.

"Maybe when I become mayor, I'll change that stupid ass fucking rule."

"Come again." The State's Attorney Andrea Myers said. If I weren't so in love with Miyani, I would definitely fuck the shit out of her. She was bad as fuck to be a white woman, and they not even my type. I needed to focus on the tasks at hand. Miyani will kill my ass if she thinks I'm sniffing up behind another bitch.

"You heard me, Ms. Lady. When I become mayor, I'm going to change a lot of the fuck shit y'all got going on in this city.

"What makes you think you would be mayor?" Governor Bragg spoke.

"Because all of you are going to endorse me. Now before you start looking crazy and talking shit, I have some-thing all of you to see. Opening my briefcase, I removed three manila envelopes. They were assigned to each of them. I placed my feet on the table and continued to smoke my blunt.

"I'll pay you whatever you want. Please don't put these pictures out there. It will destroy my family." Governor Bragg looked like he was about to pass out from shock.

"I don't want your money. It is not my desire to tell the world you like to suck dick. All I want is your endorsement for mayor in the next election. That goes for all of you. The nasty shit y'all got going on with that hoe Melissa is none of my concern. I don't want your money. All I want is the endorsement in the next election. If I have your support, then I'll be sure no one ever knows the sick shit y'all out here doing to people.

Don't look at me like that. I'm not the bad guy here. I'm just trying to make Chicago a better place for the people. So, what's it going to be?"

"We'll give you our word with only one request."

"No requests. I'm the only one around here with the

power to do that. It was nice doing business with you all. I'll be in touch." I closed my briefcase and walked off content with the results I had gotten.

Malcolm Mills kept a lot of fucking records about Melissa's business. The black book he left Miyani and Gavin was nothing compared to what Shaw had in his possession. I had to give it to that hoe Melissa. The bitch was a genius with this sex trafficking ring. Every fucking official across the nation was into this shit. It was basically modern-day slavery, except they weren't picking cotton. These motherfuckers were making billions off of pussy. Every official I had something on needed to pay the fuck up or step down from the positions they held. These niggas had to pay contributions just like the motherfuckers who want to sell drugs on the streets. You had to pay to play in my city. Now that I handled that, it was time to address this shit with Nettie.

"WHAT IS ALL this shit about? Since when do we have meetings on Saturdays?" Nettie jokingly spoke as she walked inside the warehouse.

The whole team was in attendance minus Butta and Ms. Gladys. The last thing I needed was her sitting in on this particular meeting. She has basically adopted Nettie as one of her own grandchildren. So, the reason for this meeting will have her trying to talk me out of the decision I already made. Butta's ass wasn't here because he was probably somewhere with her picking out curtains or doing some other old lady shit. I swear I believe Butta be fucking my grandma. I have never seen a trigger-happy ass nigga like him hanging with an old ass lady.

"You know we handle it immediately when shit is serious. Have a seat. We need to have a discussion." Her demeanor changed. Beads of sweat seemed to form on her forehead immediately.

"I'm just going to lay this shit on the table. Lexx and I have been fucking around. We met years back in Miami. During that time, we conceived Dakota. I'm sorry, Nettie. It wasn't some shit intended to hurt you. I'm not sure how you feel about it, but you and Lexx are *done*."

I didn't expect Gunna just to hop out the gate with everything. The nigga made sure to put the emphasis on the word done.

"I know damn well y'all didn't wake me up for this shit. Be my guest, my nigga. I've been done with Lexx. I was only fucking with her for her position at the jail. She was nothing but a pawn for the money to continue to flow. It's cool. I don't like bitches with kids anyway. There's some shit I need to get handled. Is this meeting done?"

Nettie was trying her best not to show her hand. She probably didn't give a fuck about Lexx. Finding out Gunna had snatched a bitch from her definitely had her heated, though.

"Not yet, Nettie. What the fuck is the rush? Prada asked.

"Yeah, we haven't even put shit in the air yet. That new batch of exotic just came in." Fendi added as he started rolling a blunt.

"It's not that. I just have some shit I need to get handled."

"How long have we all known each, Nettie?"

"What type of question is that, G? We've been friends since the ninth grade."

"That's a long time to be friends with someone. With

those types of years being friends, loyalty must come easy. Ain't that right, Nettie?" I took a sip of Hennessy and waited for her to respond. I could tell she was confused at how I was coming at her.

"Hell yeah, loyalty is a must. You know our motto — loyalty or death."

"It's funny you speak on death. Is that what should happen to you for fucking Niara? What? Y'all been plotting on me." I banged my fist on the table. Just that fast, my anger rose. It pissed me the fuck off knowing this bitch had played with me.

"It wasn't like that, G. I've been in love with Niara since forever. When I brought her around, I had no idea you would start fucking with her. I knew she wanted to fuck you, and I couldn't let her go, so I went along with it. I'm sorry I should have said something."

"On some real shit, Nettie. This shit got me looking at you sideways. I remember so many times coming by your crib, and she would be laid up, walking around here claiming to be kin. In reality, y'all been over there in that house starting fires with them dry ass pussies. That shit is not cool, Nettie." I tried my best not to laugh at Fendi, but he was a dumb ass nigga for saying that shit.

"What the fuck was I supposed to do? She was my bitch first."

"You were supposed to cancel that hoe if she was choosing so fucking easy. Let me find out you're in love with that hoe!"

"Fuck you, Prada!"

"Fuck your strap on wearing ass! You're fucking up the team with that shit."

"I'm fucking up the team! Nah, you niggas are the ones fucking up the team. I've been with the team forever. I've busted my ass to get pushed up in the ranks all these years, yet Miyani, Gavin, and Dream pop on the scene, and they get to rock chains. The pussy is not that good for y'all to just let them in on so much. Y'all are trying to come at me behind fucking with Niara, but I can't tell y'all shit about the women y'all chose. I would appreciate it if I have the right to choose mine."

"Right now, you're talking like a jealous ass bitch while dressed like a nigga. Let's be clear. We don't give a fuck who you choose to be with. I don't give a fuck about that cum guzzling hoe Niara. I wanted that bitch removed from around me because she wasn't to be trusted. You knew this, Nettie. I've expressed this shit to you over and over again.

You came to me several times and tried to persuade me to let that hoe back on the team, but you've been fucking her all along. How the fuck am I supposed to trust you to continue being a part of this shit? You are letting a hoe like Niara fuck up your judgment. You know what? I'm investing too much into this conversation. You need to make a choice. It's either Niara or Team Supreme."

"Fuck, Team Supreme!" Nettie took off her chain, threw it across the table, and walked off.

"Bet that!" I yelled at her as she walked off.

I poured out the rest of the Hennessy out on the floor. She was officially dead to me. I really wanted to put a bullet in Nettie's head, but she's basically family. I gave her an option I knew that she would choose. It is what the fuck it is. Ain't no love lost over this way. Obviously, Lexx can get her seat at the Team Supreme table.

Now that I had that handled that, it was time for me to gone onto the next thing that needed to be handled.

"Are you sure that was a good thing to do?" Fendi asked.

"Now you know I don't second guess shit that I do. I

gave that bitch a choice, and she made hers. That's it, and that's all. Let's get ready to handle this shit before Chanel heads back to Haiti.

"I'M surprised y'all came and picked me up. You boys haven't talked to me since I revealed I was going back to Haiti. I pray that one day you can find it in your hearts to forgive me. Please believe me when I say that you boys are more important to me than being the Queen of Coke. I've solidified business deals with some really important people over there. Not going is not an option, nor is it good for business. I'm only a plane ride away. This time I could go and come as I please. I love my kids so much that I'm giving into Versace staying here with y'all. She loves her brothers, and it's not fair that I make her go back with me. As a matter of fact, she has made it perfectly clear that she's grown and can make her own decisions. Keep an eye on my baby. If anything happens to her, that's all your asses. Now, where in the hell are we going?"

Chanel had been talking nonstop since we picked her up. After having a long conversation with our grandma, we decided not to even make her feel bad about leaving. Honestly, it felt better to give her our support instead of shit about going. In a nutshell, we all have to do what we have to do.

"You can't go back to Haiti without handling your unfinished business here. I know that you've been coming up short trying to find Melissa and Butch, but by chance, we got the drop on them."

"G? I've been looking high and low for them mother-fuckers. Where the hell did you find them?"

"Malcolm's attorney had been looking for Gavin and Miyani. He found Miyani when he saw her on the news talking about Supreme Suites. When he showed up, the nigga had black eyes and everything. Melissa had some motherfuckers beat his ass because he wouldn't hand over the money Malcolm left for Miyani and Gavin. He took that ass whooping off the loyalty he had to Malcolm. That man wanted to make sure that money got into the right hands.

She threatened to kill his family if he didn't turn everything over to her. He acted as if he didn't know where the shit was to buy him some time. I made him an offer he couldn't refuse. We had some fake documents printed up and had Shaw delivered them to an address in The Heights?"

"What the fuck is that bougie bitch doing hiding in the hood? The Heights is her old stomping grounds. She's been hiding in plain sight. She knew this was the last place anybody would look for her. Damn! How come I didn't think about coming over here?"

"I can't wait to gut Melissa like a fucking fish! That bitch has to die a painful ass death for the way she treated Gavin. I can't rest until we end her ass. This shit has been going on for too damn long."

"I'm with you, bro. It's crazy how one woman single-handedly created so much fucking chaos. It's time for The Alexander family to end this shit. As long as she's living, we will never have the peace that we need. I know this won't stop the enemies from coming but eliminating her ass would take a big weight off." It felt good to be with my brothers and my mother. We were getting ready to handle the people that fucked our family up.

After about driving for about thirty more minutes, we

ended up in the heart of the hood. The shit looked ran down as fuck. The closer we made it to the building, the more I started to see flashing lights.

"FUCK! FUCK! FUCK!" I yelled, hitting the steering wheel repeatedly. The fucking FEDS had swarmed the building. I was sick watching them bring Melissa and Butch out in handcuffs.

"How the fuck them people make it out here before us? I'm so pissed off right now. I really was ready to off that bitch, Melissa!" Prada said as he hit the back of the passenger side headrest.

"Man, G, are you sure that fucking lawyer didn't tip them people off?" Fendi asked.

"Nah! He was solid with the way that he was moving. Plus, he wanted Melissa to pay for what she did to Malcolm."

"I'm not surprised these motherfuckers had been hiding out together. Butch is one coward ass nigga to still be fucking with that scandalous ass hoe. Let's discuss this shit at home! The last thing we need is to be seen while this shit is going on. For them to be being locked up it's some bigger shit going on. Trust me. It looks like I might be staying here a little while longer. I was only going back to Haiti if Melissa's ass was dead. We're just going to have to get at her from the inside. This is just a monkey wrench that was thrown in the game. I'm going to reach out to some people and see what's going on."

This shit just keeping get worse. I've never had such a damn tough time trying to kill someone. It's as if this bitch just kept slipping through my fingers. As I headed back home, I became so damn angry. Why was it so damn hard for me to get rid of this bitch? She can be touched behind the wall, but I would much rather touch her out here.

On the drive back, all I could think about was Miyani. I promised her I was going to get rid of Melissa. Now, I have to go back home and tell her she got away from my ass again. This shit is so frustrating. That lady caused Miyani too much fucking pain to still be breathing. I know she'll understand. It's just that it doesn't sit right with me to let her down. She has never let me down. That's why I'm going so fucking hard with trying to get rid of Melissa's ass. It's just time to come up with another course of action.

SIXTEEN
MIYANI

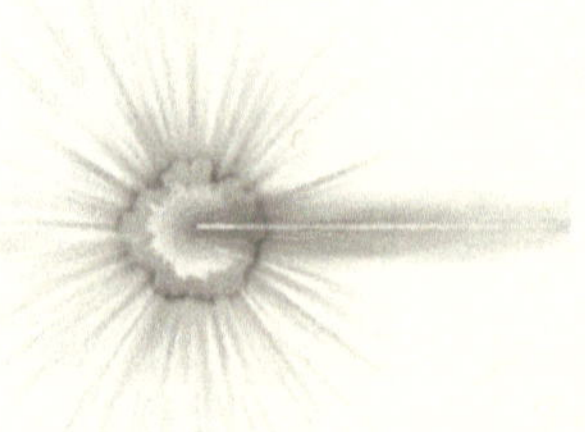

After a long day of getting the girls ready for their next recital, I was beat. All I wanted to do was get home so that I could take a nice hot bath, plus I missed my son. I had been away from G-Baby all day long. All he does is cry, but I love being with my crybaby. I never knew I could love someone as much as I do my son. Givenchy says I'm going to make him soft. I don't care. I just want to give him all the love I have to give. That love from a parent is everything. I know how it feels to be neglected by a parent. As long as I have blood flowing through my veins, I'm going to make sure my children feel loved. Being a mom to him and Gianna completes me. I never thought I would see the day where I would race home to my family.

Hearing the siren and seeing the flashing lights made me quickly pull to the side of the road. I immediately reached for my license and registration. I really didn't understand why I was being pulled over in the first place. I hadn't run any signs or lights, and I had my proper signals on as well as my seatbelt. This officer had no reason to stop me. I damn near jumped out of my skin the way he banged on my window.

"License and registration, please!

"Why am I being pulled over? I didn't do anything, officer."

I quickly handed my documents to him. He quickly walked off, and I observed him getting back inside of his patrol car. I bit down on my bottom lip nervously because it started to take too long.

After about ten minutes of waiting, I observed another patrol car pull up. At that time, an officer and a K-9 dog started walking toward my car. I noticed the officer who had pulled me over started walking with them. My heart felt like it was about to jump out of my chest. I didn't understand why they needed a dog. Something was off with this traffic stop. I regretted not calling Givenchy when the officer first pulled me over. Now it was too late because they had come back to the car.

"Step out of the car, ma'am!"

"For what?"

"Please don't resist! Step out of the car, ma'am!" This time he spoke with anger in his voice.

I quickly got out of the car and walked me off to the side afraid he might shoot me. The dog immediately started to go crazy sniffing by the trunk. I knew that dog had to be fucked up or something. There were no drugs of any kind in my car.

"Jackpot! It's must be over twenty keys in here."

"What! No! No! Somebody put that shit in there. Please let me call my fiancé!" I was crying begging and pleading, but he forcibly put me in cuffs. He was reading me my rights, but it's as if my whole body was numb. Somebody had planted that shit inside of my trunk. Who in the fuck would do some shit like that to me? On the ride to the jail, all I could do is think about Givenchy and the kids. What would they do with me being locked up? This shit was so fucked up. *Why does bad shit keep happening?*

ONE WEEK **Later**

I was about to lose my fucking mind sitting in the jail cell. Shit was all bad. The judge held me without bail. There was no telling how long I was about to be in here. The whole family had been trying to keep me calm each time I called. All I want to do is go home to G and the kids. I'm not supposed to be locked up. Givenchy needed to handle this shit so that I could get the fuck outta here. To make matters worse, my ass is knocked up again. I found out when I came through intake. There was no way I could have a baby behind bars.

"Let's go, Mills. You have a special visit!" I hurried up and got up from my bunk. Givenchy told me he was going to get us a visit. All I need to do is see him and touch him. It will make me feel so better about the situation.

"Do you know if it's my fiancé?"

"Sorry. I don't know who it is."

We continued to walk down a long corridor until we

came to a small door. He uncuffed me and basically pushed me inside. The moment I locked eyes with Melissa in the same orange jumpsuit as mine, I knew this was about to be some bullshit.

"My have the mighty fallen. Look at you, daughter, you're a reflection of your mother." She laughed as she flamed up a Newport.

"I'm nothing like you."

"Yes, you are. That's the problem. You're walking around thinking you're better than me when you're really just like me. I mean, look, we're dressed just alike."

"Orange fits you just well. Let me out of here!" I started banging on the door, but it never opened. Melissa got up from where she was sitting and got so far in my face our noses were damn near touching.

"Do you think I built my life just so that you could make it crumble? From the moment I birthed your ass, I knew you would fuck my life up. Now, look at you. Talk that big shit now about what your man can do! Newsflash, that nigga don't run shit in here. As a matter of fact, I run this whole tier, and you will fall in line like the rest of the bitches. You want to go against me for Team Supreme! Game on, daughter! Always remember, I brought you in this world, and I have the power to take you out!"

Before I could say anything, the door opened and in walked about four female inmates. I didn't really have a chance to scream or do anything. They all just started beating the fuck out of me. I tried my best to fight back, but I was outnumbered. It seemed like the punches and kicks would not stop coming. I could feel blood dripping into my eyes, so everything was blurry. I felt myself giving up and just falling to the floor. I could hear G in my head repeating his motto.

Chin up and chest the fuck out!

It gave me the strength to stay standing for a little while longer. I fought like hell trying not to let them get me down. All the fight I had in me was gone when one of them pulled out a blade and sliced my face. I hit the floor like a ton of bricks, and the beating stopped. As I stared into Melissa's dark eyes, I vowed to survive and make her pay for everything she's done to me. This *Hood Supreme* shit was about to get real fucking heavy around this motherfucker!!!!

TO BE CONTINUED

Coming March

LETTER FROM THE AUTHOR!!!

I know that in the last installment I said that Part 3 was the last. However, the majority of readers begged me for more. I honestly didn't see this book going past two parts. This title went to another storyline that I had been sitting on for two years.

I finally decided to write it and changed the entire concept. I had no idea this book would get the praise it has. Please forgive me if this route for another installment upsets you. I promise it will release in March!

Remember, there is a method to my madness in regard to the way I plot and leave you hanging. All roads lead to something greater!!!!

Text Shan to 22828 to stay up to date with new releases, sneak peeks, contest, and more....